LAST CHANCE

A ROBYN HUNTER MYSTERY

NORAH McCLINTOCK

MINNEAPOLIS

First U.S. edition published in 2012 by Lerner Publishing Group, Inc.

Darby Creek
A division of Lerner Publishing Group, Inc.
241 First Avenue North
Minneapolis, MN 55401 U.S.A.

Website address: www.lernerbooks.com

The image in this book is used with the permission of: Front Cover: © Photo by Melissa Keizer - www.KeizGoesBoom.com/ Flickr/Getty Images.

Main body text set in Janson Text Lt Std 11.5/15.
Typeface provided by Linotype AG.

Library of Congress Cataloging-in-Publication Data

McClintock, Norah.
    Last chance / by Norah McClintock.
        p.   cm. — (Robyn Hunter mysteries ; #1)
    ISBN: 978-0-7613-8311-6 (lib. bdg. : alk. paper)
    [1. Mystery and detective stories. 2. Juvenile delinquency—
Fiction.] I. Title.
PZ7.M478414184Las 2012
[Fic]—dc23   2011018832

Manufactured in the United States of America
1 – SB – 12/31/11

To my favorite
non-dog-owning
dog lover

CHAPTER ONE

My father was grinning. He'd been grinning ever since he had arrived at the police station. I was beginning to wish I hadn't called him. But what choice did I have? I'd been arrested. It was either call my father, who knows a lot of cops, as well as the ins and outs of arrests and (I hoped) releases. Or call my mother, who, as a criminal lawyer, has defended all kinds of people who've gotten themselves into trouble with the law.

I chose my father for the simple reason that unlike my mother, he doesn't freak out every time something unfortunate happens to me. True, he was enjoying the details of my, um, mishap far too much. But I had complete confidence that he could get me home again with minimum fuss.

Unfortunately, my friend Billy—whom I blamed for my arrest—had decided to do me a huge favor.

He'd called my mother.

My mom bustled into the police station, looking one-half lawyerly and efficient, even on a Saturday (she'd been meeting with a client), and one-half motherly and concerned. Her eyes scanned the room for me but landed squarely on my father, who is impossible to miss because he's so tall. And, of course, there's that grin of his.

My mother looked annoyed when she saw him. My parents broke up a few years ago. My mother says that she has moved on. My father . . . well, he's either still in love with her or he's perpetrating one of the longest-running practical jokes in history.

Mom shook her head before approaching the sergeant sitting behind the desk. He nodded in the direction of a grim-faced woman who was standing all the way on the other side of the room, as far from me as she could get. I didn't blame her. My mother glanced at the woman. Then she straightened her shoulders and came toward my father and me as if she were marching into battle. *"Arrested?"* she said. "Really, Robyn!"

My father chuckled. "Relax, Patti," he said, which, as usual, made my mother seethe. She hates being called Patti. She reminds my father over and over again that her name is Patricia. "It was an accident."

"Your daughter gets arrested and you think it's funny?" she said.

"Well, you have to admit—" my father began.

"It's not funny, Dad," I said, for about the millionth time.

My mother turned her eyes on me. "Tell me in your own words exactly what you did to that woman."

"I didn't do anything," I said. What I meant was that I hadn't done anything *on purpose*. "Dad's right. It was an accident."

"The police don't arrest people for accidents, Robyn," my mother said. "What happened?"

"I was at a rally," I began.

"A *protest* rally," my father said.

"A *peaceful* protest rally," I said, glaring at him. I turned to my mother. "We were demonstrating against the use of animals in product testing."

"Peaceful," my mother repeated. "Can you tell me why you broke a store window during a *peaceful* protest?"

Uh-oh. The sergeant must have given her a run-down of what had happened. Or maybe Billy had filled her in over the phone.

"Well, technically—" I began.

"The window is either broken or it isn't, Robyn," my mother said. When it comes to questioning, my mother is all lawyer. She doesn't like evasion. She doesn't like ambiguity.

"The window got broken," I said. "But it's complicated."

My mother waited.

"I was trying to stop Bil—" I broke off abruptly. Maybe Billy hadn't told her everything. If he hadn't, I didn't want to get him into trouble.

"You're going to blame Billy?" my mother said. Okay, so maybe he had told her everything. Well, why not?

My mother liked Billy—who didn't?—and he knew it. He came across as a sweet-faced, gentle-natured vegan who would never hurt another living soul, two-footed or four-footed.

"No," I said. I had thought about focusing her attention on the fact that I had gone to the protest only because Billy had badgered me and pointing out that it had all started when I tried to stop Billy from throwing something nasty at one of the security guards who worked at the office building where we had held our protest. But I could see now that it wasn't a good idea. "It was just one of those things, Mom. We didn't have a problem with that woman's store. It just happens to be next door to the cosmetics company that we were protesting against. And this security guard started giving us a hard time. He was really getting rough, Mom."

"Oh," she said. "So you're telling me that a security guard who was just doing his job is at fault here?"

"I don't think Robbie is blaming anyone," my father said. "She's just trying to explain."

My mother's eyes flicked over to my father. "She's fifteen, Mac. She doesn't need you to run interference for her."

Actually, I appreciated his efforts. I continued my testimony, er, explanation.

"I was holding a pole at one side of this huge protest banner that Billy and his friends had made. When I saw what Billy was going to do, all I could think about was stopping him before *he* got into trouble." The look my mother gave me told me that she was finding it hard to imagine Billy in trouble. "So I lunged at him and managed to get the plastic baggie out of his hand."

At the mention of the baggie, my father started to chuckle again. I tried to ignore him.

"I can see how it might have *looked like* I was pointing the end of the pole at the window. I can even see how it might have looked like I was trying to break the window. But that's not what I was trying to do. Honest. You know me. I would never do anything like that." She looked doubtful. "Anyway, the window got broken and then a woman came out of the store"—the store owner, as it turned out—"and started yelling at me. And I was so stunned at what had happened that I forgot that I was still holding the baggie." My father stifled a chortle. "Then she grabbed me, which I wasn't expecting, and well, I sort of let go of the baggie." My father chuckled again. It wasn't my fault that the baggie wasn't very strong and that it hadn't been securely closed, but I didn't tell my mother that. She would just think I was trying to lay the blame off again. "I didn't mean for it to happen, Mom."

She looked at me for a moment. Then she said, "Let's go."

I stared at her.

"We're leaving?" I said. Relief washed over me. I couldn't wait to get out of the police station.

"We're going to talk to the plaintiff," my mother said. "We're going to see if we can work something out."

"Good idea," my father said. "Let's see what we can do."

"*We?*" my mother said, giving my father a sharp look. "I think I can handle this, Mac." Meaning, *Stay out of it, Mac.*

"Are you sure?" my father said, looking over at the still-grim-looking woman across the room. "Because I've had a lot of experience—"

My mother bristled. "*I've* had a lot of experience too," she said. "Come on, Robyn."

I glanced at my father. He shrugged and stayed put. I trailed my mother toward the woman who was glowering at me.

My mother smiled at the woman as she introduced herself. The woman did not smile back. My mother nudged me, and I apologized. When I had finished, Mom explained that it had all been an unfortunate accident. The woman was not moved. I couldn't really blame her. I think I would have stayed mad for a week if someone dropped on me what I had dropped on her.

"If you don't press charges, Robyn will be more than happy to make restitution," my mother said. Although it wasn't the main part of her practice, my mother sometimes dealt with youth criminal law cases. A lot of time she ended up negotiating alternate measures. She was good at it. "She'll work in your store. For free."

The woman took a step backward when she heard this proposition. Clearly she didn't want a vandal—and worse—anywhere near her store.

"Or she could do volunteer work," my mother said quickly. To give her credit, she was trying hard to save my day. "Do you have a favorite charity? If so, Robyn would be more than happy to volunteer on your behalf, wouldn't you, Robyn?"

I nodded. The truth was, I was embarrassed by what had happened, embarrassed at having been packed into the back of a police car, and embarrassed that the first person I'd seen at the police station was a friend of my father's. I would have agreed to anything if it got me out of there.

Finally, *mercifully* (I thought at the time), the woman said yes, she had a favorite charity.

Wonderful, my mother said.

It was an animal shelter, the woman said.

I tried to keep a smile on my face. After all, the woman's window had been broken and her clothes had been ruined, thanks to me. Well, thanks to Billy, whom I had been trying to prevent from getting arrested. And even though she still smelled faintly foul—despite having washed up and changed her clothes—she was willing to give me a break. It was only smart to appear as grateful as possible.

"You mean, an animal shelter that looks after dogs?" I said.

"Dogs, cats, rabbits, the usual," the woman said.

"I think Robyn might prefer some other type of charity work," my mother said in the brisk, I'm-sure-we-can-reach-a-compromise voice that's become second nature to her since she started practicing law. "She isn't comfortable around dogs."

"Oh?" the woman said. "Isn't that too bad. Perhaps she would be more comfortable appearing in court."

My mother didn't even look at me before she said, "But, of course, she'll be glad to volunteer at the animal shelter anyway, if that's what you want."

"It is," the woman said, adding, "I would have thought that someone who takes to the streets to demand humane treatment for animals would at least *like* the animals in question."

I supposed she had a point.

My mother agreed that I would volunteer at the shelter for the rest of the summer. I groaned. Both my mother and the woman turned to look at me. I forced myself to smile, even though *volunteering* meant that my original rest-of-the-summer plan—three weeks at a cottage up north with Morgan, one of my two best friends—was evaporating in front of my eyes like dew on a mid-July morning. My mother quickly put the agreement in writing and had us both sign it. The woman said she would talk to the chair of the shelter's fund-raising committee—a personal friend of hers— who would make all the arrangements. Someone from the shelter would call me later to discuss the details. And then I was free.

Free and doomed.

.   .   .

"You can't come up here at all?" Morgan said when I called her to break the news. She sounded even more disappointed than I was.

"Sorry," I said. "But either I volunteer or the woman presses charges. If she does, my mom says I'd probably end up with community service, anyway. At least this way I don't end up with a criminal record too."

When I told Morgan where I was volunteering, she laughed—for longer than was strictly necessary, in my opinion.

Billy, bless his heart, did not laugh. When I called him, he apologized. Abjectly. He said, "I wasn't going to throw that baggie at the guard. It didn't even belong to me. It was Evan's. It was his idea. He said it was a good way to make a real splash. When I saw that he was actually going to throw it, I grabbed it from him, you know, so that he wouldn't get into trouble—"

"*What?*" I couldn't believe it. I had grabbed that stupid baggie out of Billy's hands to stop Billy from getting arrested and had ended up saving Evan Wilson instead. And I didn't even like Evan! He's one of those ultra-serious activists who make everyone else feel guilty about *everything*. "But I thought—"

"I would never do anything like that," Billy said. "I'm not like Evan. You know that."

Correction: I *should* have known. Billy would protest himself hoarse for a cause he believed in, but he would never harm another living creature—including a human being. Nor was he the type to damage

9

property. Billy believed in reason, persuasion, and education.

"In that case, Evan is the one who should be apologizing to me," I said.

"Actually, he thinks you're a hero," Billy said.

"He thinks you were going to throw it. He told me he was impressed. He didn't think you had it in you—you know, because of your parents. He says it really made him reevaluate you, Robyn."

Uh-huh.

"In fact, the other reason I called..." He paused. He sounded uncomfortable. If he had been talking to me face-to-face, I bet he would have been flushed and would have avoided my eyes. "Evan was wondering... He asked me if maybe I could find out if you—"

"No way, Billy," I said.

"But I—" he spluttered. "I—"

"If you're trying to find out if I'd be interested in going out with Evan, the answer is no. Billy, how could you even ask?"

"I'm sorry," Billy said. I had no doubt that he was. "Sorry about everything, Robyn. Especially about the volunteering part."

I told him it was okay—but I only said it because he was my other best friend.

CHAPTER **TWO**

"If you want my opinion," my father said on Monday morning, "I'd say your situation is what they call ironic."

I didn't want his opinion. But my father is the kind of person who is generous with his views. You never have to ask—he always volunteers them. He was sitting at the huge oak dining table in loft where he lives. The loft is located in what used to be a carpet factory in what used to be a seedy part of the city. The area is trendy now. The first floor houses a hugely popular gourmet restaurant, La Folie. The second floor consists of six apartments. Dad occupies the entire third floor. He owns the building too. He inherited it from his uncle before I was born, did nothing with it for years, and then converted it after he quit being a cop a few years ago. He could live off what he makes as a landlord. Could but doesn't.

"How exactly is my situation ironic?" I said.

"Well," he said, "you were protesting the use of animals in product testing, correct?"

"Correct."

"Specifically, the use of cats and dogs, correct?"

I nodded. I could see where this was heading.

"Take a dog-friendly cause, mix in a little dog poop, and the result?" my father said. "My dog-phobic daughter ends up being literally thrown to the dogs."

I could imagine him telling this story to all of his friends. He'd probably even make the rounds of the tables at La Folie downstairs. According to my father, if you've got a good story, you practically have an obligation to share it, even with complete strangers.

"You call it irony, Dad," I said. "I call it your fault."

My father raised an eyebrow and lowered his cup of coffee. *"My* fault?"

"You're the one who always says that a person has to stand for something."

My father stands for law and order. Since retiring from the police department, he's been running an enormously successful private security business. I stand for animal rights—among other things. I believe that all living creatures deserve equal consideration on our planet. That's why I'm a vegetarian. It's also why I'm against inhumane treatment of animals. All animals. Even dogs. After all, you can't be against human encroachment into the natural habitats of lions and tigers and grizzly bears (which I am) and think that it's perfectly fine to blind or even kill a dog by exposing it to high levels of chemicals used in testing hair dye or mascara. Yes, I'm afraid (terrified) of dogs. But I'm perfectly willing to live and let live. I'm just not always sure that our canine so-called friends share that philosophy.

Some people, dog lovers like Morgan and Billy and my father, think my extreme nervousness around dogs is the result of childhood trauma. They're right. It is. They think I should get over it. Easy for them to say. They weren't attacked by a German shepherd when they were eight years old. From what I can remember and what I have been told, the attack was unprovoked. It was also terrifying. I ended up in the emergency ward, getting stitches · in a part of my anatomy that made it next to impossible for me to sit down for the better part of a week. I got into the habit of sleeping on my stomach at about that time.

Other people—my mother, for example—think my aversion to big, mean-looking dogs is one of my more admirable qualities. Common sense, she calls it. She is 100 percent opposed to people keeping what she believes are vicious dogs. Of course, this may be because of the trauma *she* suffered when she saw the German shepherd sink his teeth into my posterior. She says she had to hit it with her purse twice before it left me alone, and even then, it was the dog's owner—who had been at the other end of the park when the dog attacked me—who actually pulled the dog away. My mother had wanted to hit him too, but even before she went to law school, she still knew the difference between self-defense and assault.

As far as volunteering at an animal shelter, well, I'm no fool. I knew what kind of dog gets dumped at an animal shelter—the kind that nobody wants. The problem dogs. My father knew it too, despite his amusement. I think that's why he was nice to me on the drive out to the animal shelter. He didn't insist on blaring '70s headbanger rock full blast on his Porsche's sound system the way he usually does. Instead, he offered to let me program the music and didn't complain when I chose the sounds of silence. Not the Simon and Garfunkel song but actual sounds of silence.

The German shepherd's snarling face hovered in my imagination as my father pulled into the animal shelter's parking lot. The shelter was located on the outskirts of the city and was surrounded by summer-scorched fields planted with "For Sale" signs. My father killed the engine of his Porsche and turned to look at me. He had never backed down from anything in his life, so when he gave one of his speeches about facing and conquering your fears, you knew he wasn't talking about anything he hadn't done himself. Whatever else he was—and Mom had a few theories—he wasn't a hypocrite. He wasn't totally insensitive, either. He looked at the low-slung building shimmering in the early-August heat, frowned, and said, "Are you sure you're okay with this, Robbie?"

"I'm fine," I said.

I was not fine. I was scared. But I told myself the same thing I had tried to convince myself of the previous night: I had nothing to worry about. The shelter's director had told me that I'd be working with computers, not dogs. She also told me—after I asked—that all the dogs were kept in kennels and that when they weren't in their kennels, they were always with either a volunteer dog walker or a staff member. So I was looking at a low-risk situation, as my father might have said. I got out of the car, stared at the unfamiliar building, and gulped back the fear that was burning the back of my throat.

I heard a soft whirring sound beside me as my father lowered the driver's side window.

"Hey," he said, crooking a finger at me. I stepped closer to the car and felt the chill of the air-conditioned interior. My father crooked his finger again, and I bent down. He kissed my cheek. "You're going to be fine," he said. "It's an office job. Office jobs are all the same. Maybe someone swipes your lunch out of the fridge. No sweat, right?"

Perspiration trickled down the back of my neck. I offered him a shaky smile.

"That's my girl," he said. "It's going to be a piece of cake. I mean, what's the worst that could happen?"

I discovered the answer to that question right after I watched my father drive away.

CHAPTER **THREE**

When I turned toward the main entrance to the animal shelter, I found myself facing a massive ebony beast with dead-looking eyes and a mouthful of teeth that screamed, "Born to bite."

I happen to know *a lot* about vicious dogs. It's my obsession. For example, I know that there are nearly five million recorded instances of dog bites every year in the United States alone. I know that one million of these bites are serious, *every* year, and that twenty people die from them, *every* year. I know that more than half the victims are under the age of eighteen, that dog bites are the leading cause of facial disfigurement among North American children. Also, the number of dogs has increased by 2 percent in the past ten years while the number of reported dog bites has jumped by 37 percent. So whenever I see a dog off a leash with no human nearby, I react exactly as I did when I found myself face-to-face with the black monster in front of the animal shelter: I stop dead in my tracks, look down at the ground, and mentally review the rules on dog-bite avoidance—which I also know.

Rule number one: Always assume that a dog that doesn't know you may view you as an intruder or a threat. Especially assume this if the dog is growling at you and if the dog's tail is not, repeat *not*, wagging.

Rule number two: Never turn your back to a dog and run away. A dog's natural instinct is to chase you and catch you—and then treat you like a chew toy.

Rule number three: If you are approached by a dog that you think might attack you (for example, a massive ebony beast with dead-looking eyes and a mouthful of teeth that scream, "Born to bite"), remain motionless with your hands at your sides and avoid eye contact with the dog. After the dog loses interest in you (which you pray it will), slowly back away until it is out of sight. Try to hide your fear.

Rule number four: If the dog attacks, feed it your jacket, your purse, your bicycle (the book I read actually said this—your bicycle!), or anything else that you can put between you and the dog.

And finally, rule number five: If you fall or are knocked to the ground, curl into a ball with your hands over your ears. Do *not* move. Do *not* scream. Do *not* roll around. Apparently, this will only encourage the dog to attack.

So there I was, standing in front of an animal shelter that should (theoretically) have been filled with people who not only love animals but who also know exactly how to handle them. Apparently none of those people happened to be looking out a window. None of them saw me. None of them came to my rescue.

The dog stood in front of me, blocking my way and growling. I fought the urge to call (scream) for help and stood motionless, per rule number three. My hands hung at my sides. They were also motionless. I didn't want the dog to mistake my fingers for juicy, beckoning sausages. I stared at the ground because, apparently, locking eyes with an aggressive dog is the canine version of slapping an adversary across the face with a glove—the dog thinks you're challenging it to a duel.

I waited for the dog to lose interest in me.

It didn't.

I stood there, barely breathing. I tried to block out murderous thoughts about Billy and his peaceful protest and instead tried to get into the moment, into the Zen, of being a statue. *I am granite*, I told myself. *I cannot move. I will not move. And if I am bitten, I will not bleed. I will feel no pain. Because I am granite.*

The dog made a sound that some people might describe as barking, but barking didn't begin to capture it. This wasn't *arf-arf* or *bow-wow*. This was the sound of thunder being channeled through a canine throat. I jumped. Then I immediately thought: *stupid, stupid, stupid! You know the rules. You should not have moved.*

The dog knew the rules too. When I jumped, he charged.

A single thought flashed through my brain like a comet in a midnight sky: *Run.*

Run now.

Run fast.

Then I thought about that brute chasing me, and catching me, and I stayed put.

I tried not to look at the dog.

I tried not to panic.

And then a miracle happened.

The dog aborted its charge less than a couple feet away.

Maybe the rules really worked?

Then someone shouted: "Orion!"

Finally. A human being. *A rescuer.*

"Orion! Come!"

The dog stopped growling and turned its head to look at the person who had called his name—a teenage boy who looked like the human equivalent of the animal in front of me. His hair was as black as the dog's coat. A hairline scar cut diagonally across his right cheek, from close to the top of his nose to close to the bottom of his ear. Despite the intense heat of the afternoon, he was wearing a black T-shirt, black jeans, and black boots that would have been happy nestled on the footrests of a motorcycle. The dog looked at the boy, but it didn't back off. On the plus side, it didn't come any closer to me. Instead, it stood its ground until the boy came over and snapped a leash onto its collar. A chain leash, I noticed. The kind a dog couldn't chew through.

Now that the dog was restrained, I took a good long look at it. It was 50 percent teeth and 100 percent muscle, and it was straining so hard on the leash that the boy's biceps bulged as he held it. I hoped that the boy was as strong as he looked.

"I'm sorry," he said. "He got away from me."

"No problem," I said, my voice trembling. No problem? *Big* problem. If this boy was responsible for the dog, he shouldn't have let it get away from him. On the other hand, he sounded genuinely apologetic and, despite his all-black wardrobe, he was kind of hot. His eyes were an amazing shade of blue that verged on purple. I had only ever seen eyes like that once before and that was back when nothing about boys interested me, including their eyes. "Is he your dog?" I asked.

The boy shook his head. "He lives here," he said, nodding at the shelter. "But don't worry, he wouldn't have bitten you. Orion looks way scarier than he actually is."

I glanced at the dog again and was *not* comforted.

The boy scratched the dog behind one ear. The dog bowed its head to expose more head-scratching surface. The boy smiled. The dog dropped its butt to the ground. Then it crouched and rolled over, begging for more. The boy obliged. While I watched the two of them, I got a strange feeling, as if something about this was familiar. The boy straightened up and looked at me again. He frowned.

"Is something wrong?" I said.

He shook his head.

"Do you work here?"

The question seemed to startle him, but he looked pleased. "No," he said.

"So you're a volunteer?"

His smile faded. "Not exactly." He thought a moment. "Well, sometimes."

Not exactly? What did that mean? And *sometimes*, but not *now*? And why was I getting a weird déjà-vu feeling when I looked at him?

"I'm Nick," he said.

The feeling became overpowering. Now I was almost positive I knew him, but I couldn't figure out how. He didn't seem like the kind of guy I'd forget.

"Hey," someone called. We both turned. A stocky guy with brush-cut hair, wearing relaxed-fit jeans and a collared knit shirt, was standing at one corner of the building. "D'Angelo, get a move on. You're holding us up!"

D'Angelo? *Nick D'Angelo?* I peered at him as he turned toward the man. Then it hit me like a kick to the stomach.

What was the worst that could happen, my father had asked.

I had been here for all of five minutes, and so far I had made the journey from bad to worse.

Next stop . . .

CHAPTER **FOUR**

Nick D'Angelo frowned at me again. "Do I know you?" he said

"Uh, no, I don't think so," I said. "This is my first day."

"Hey, D'Angelo!" the man called again, making the name sound like a command.

Nick took a last look at me before saying, "Heel." As I watched him and the dog disappear around the side of the building, I thought, *Why me?* Better yet: Why him? Of all the people from my past, why, oh why, did I have to run into Nick D'Angelo? What was he even doing here? He didn't work here, but he said he wasn't *exactly* a volunteer either. Maybe he was like me, a "voluntold"— told by someone else that he *had* to volunteer. Given what I knew about him, that was a real possibility.

I glanced at my watch. Five minutes late—on my first day. I hurried through the main door of the animal shelter and approached the reception desk.

The woman sitting behind the desk smiled up at me.

"I'm here to see Kathy Lennox," I said.

The woman asked me my name and told me to take a seat. A moment later, another woman bustled into the reception area. She was small and dressed casually in light summer pants and a cotton blouse.

"Robyn?" she said, flashing me a sunny smile and thrusting out a hand. "I'm Kathy." We shook hands. She introduced me to Cindy, the receptionist, and then she said, "Let me give you the five-minute tour before I show you what you're going to be doing here."

I followed her around the sprawling building, which was a maze of corners and corridors. Kathy introduced me to a lot of people whose names I promptly forgot.

"Don't worry," Kathy said. "After a couple of days, you'll have everyone sorted out."

She led me to a door that opened to a long corridor. On the floor near the door was a basin of what looked like water with a hemp doormat in it. A wet towel lay on the floor beside the basin.

"We had a viral outbreak here a few weeks ago," Kathy said. She stepped into the basin and squished up and down on the mat. "This is bleach. Anyone going into and out of any of the animal areas has to disinfect the soles of their shoes. We think we've got it under control, but we're going to be careful for another few days." She stepped out of the basin and stood aside for me. I squished up and down and understood why I had been instructed to wear old shoes.

As we walked past another hall, Kathy pointed and said, "That's the animal clinic down there." We passed a store that sold pet food and pet equipment; a large laundry room filled with washing machines, clothes dryers, and shelves piled high with towels; and, finally, a kitchen where the animals' meals were prepared. All of these areas were bustling with activity. I had never been in an animal shelter before. I had never considered all the things that went into making sure that animals were healthy, clean, and properly fed.

We turned a corner and Kathy pushed open a door.

"This used to be an office," she said. Stacks of metal cages filled most of the room. Each cage contained either a kitten or a cat. "We have three times more animals in here right now than we're really equipped for," Kathy said. "A lot of them are cats."

And a lot of them weren't. I peeked into another used-to-be-an-office and saw rabbits, mice, a white rat and, in a fenced-in enclosure under a window, an enormous white . . .

"Is that a duck?" I said.

"Two ducks," Kathy said, pointing to a second duck that I hadn't noticed squatting in one corner of the enclosure.

"Do you get a lot of them?" I said.

She sighed. "We get everything. If an animal has been mistreated or abandoned and if someone brings it in or reports it, we take it. If it's sick, we treat it. We treat an animal twice for whatever is wrong with it. If it doesn't recover . . ." She shrugged, a slow, sad roll of her shoulders. "We have so many cats because people don't get them spayed or neutered. We have rabbits because people get them for their kids at Easter or buy them when they're cute little bunnies. They don't realize how big they get or how much care they need."

"Will they all get adopted?" I said.

This earned me another slow shrug. "We do pretty well with cats and kittens," she said. "Dogs, too. But adult rabbits?" She left the question unanswered.

When we reached the end of the corridor, she pushed open a door that led outside. We walked along a path to the other part of the building, immersed the soles of our shoes in another basin of bleach, and entered what Kathy called the original animal wing. The minute Kathy pushed open the door, we were assailed with barking.

Dogs.

Two whole corridors filled with them. They were housed in kennels—fairly large enclosures with chain-link doors and ceiling-high dividers between them. Each kennel contained one dog, one bowl of water, and one blanket for the dog to lie on. Like the rest of the shelter, the kennels were spotless. They held every type of dog imaginable—cocker spaniels, collies, German shepherds . . .

"That's a pig," I said, surprised. At least, it looked like a pig.

Kathy nodded, "A pot-bellied pig," she said. "They were popular a few years ago."

It was no mystery how the animal had got its name. The stout, black-haired creature looked like a small barrel on legs. Its head was deep into its food dish and—

"It's wagging its tail," I said. "Just like a dog."

I tiptoed closer to get a better look—and leaped back again when the dogs on either side of the pig hurled themselves at the chain-link gates of their kennels, barking. I looked at Kathy and then back at the two dogs. Both were a tawny brown color and had strong, muscular bodies. They could have been twins.

"Are those—?"

"Pit bulls," Kathy said.

My heart jackhammered in my chest. I made a note-to-self: take the long way around this room. Better yet: stay in the office part of the shelter.

We continued on through the building. Kathy hadn't been kidding about how many felines called the shelter their (temporary) home. A lot of the cat cages had cards taped to them that said, "Adopted." I had seen some of those cards in the dog area, but a lot more dog kennels had signs posted to them that said, "Not ready for adoption."

"Some of the animals, especially the dogs, have to be prepared for adoption," Kathy said. Before I could ask her what she meant, someone called her from the end of the corridor. She excused herself for a moment. When she returned, she said, "I'd better get you settled."

We went back the way we had come. Kathy beckoned to a woman whom she introduced as Janet and who followed us back to the office part of the shelter.

"Janet will get you up and running," Kathy said. "I'll check in on you later. If you need anything, I'm in the office right next to yours."

Janet showed me to an office that was small enough to qualify as a closet. Somehow a computer table had been wedged inside. On the table were a computer, a telephone, and a box of papers.

"I know it's not much," Janet said. "To be honest, it used to be a file room. But at least it has four walls, a door that closes, and a window that opens."

It did not, however, have an extra chair, so Janet had to hunch over me while she showed me what she wanted me to do. I was so busy paying attention and taking notes that I barely had time to think about Nick D'Angelo. If I were lucky, I wouldn't run into him again.

. . .

"Well, how was it?" my mother asked. She had just come through the door and still had her keys and her briefcase in her hand. "They didn't make you work with dogs, did they?" She sounded even more worried than I had felt getting out of my father's car that morning.

I shook my head. "It was just like they told me on the phone," I said. "I'm working on a computer."

The worry vanished from my mother's eyes, which are a stunning shade of aquamarine. I always thought it was unfair that I hadn't inherited her coloring. My eyes are the same lead gray as my father's.

I told my mother that I would be entering names and addresses into a database, although Kathy might need me to do odd jobs every now and then.

"Did your father pick you up like he promised, or did you end up having to take the bus?" she asked later, over dinner. My father had spent nearly twenty years as a police officer and since retiring from the force had built an enormously successful business. But my mother always talked about him as if he were an overgrown teenager who couldn't be trusted to do his chores. Probably because he had missed more than a few birthday and anniversary celebrations. To be fair, that was usually because of work.

"Dad was right on time," I said.

"Did he say anything about me?"

"No."

My mother studied me for a moment. "You haven't told him about Ted, have you, Robyn?"

Ted Gold was the man my mother had been seeing for nearly five months. She seemed to like him a lot. I didn't blame her. He was nice. In fact, I liked him a lot too, which was why, this time, I had resisted the urge to mention him to my father the way I'd mentioned other men my mother had gone out with. It was also why, this time, I could react to her question with sincere indignation.

"Of course I haven't," I said. "A promise is a promise." My mother was fanatical about keeping her personal life private from my father—for good reason. "I don't think he even suspects that you're seeing someone." Why would he? He usually relies on me to volunteer that type of information.

"Well, if he asks, don't say a word. I don't want him harassing Ted the way he harassed Anthony, Patrick, and Chris."

Anthony, Patrick, and Chris are other men my mother has been out with. My father didn't actually harass them so much as he'd *chatted* with them. And in all fairness, that had been during the first year that he and my mother were separated (but still technically married). Right after the separation, my mother had gone through an intense period of dating that had only lasted a few months. I think she wanted to purge my father from her system. That period had coincided with my father being in complete denial about the separation, which is why, I think, he'd behaved the way he had. He'd grilled me for information about who my mother was seeing, and I had happily supplied it (I think I was in denial too). And then he'd had *little talks* with the men in my mother's life.

The men involved learned that my father is a big guy, in great shape (for someone his age), with a forceful personality. They learned that he was an ex-cop with a lot of friends on the police force. They also learned that he was in private security now. My father told them that they would probably be surprised at how much information one person can find out about another person if he knows where to look. He told them that the main thing he's learned by being in the security business is that everybody, but *everybody*, has something that they'd prefer to keep secret from the rest of the world. My father's personality, along with his access to a wealth of information, had alienated the affections of Anthony, a professor of English literature (a pretentious bore, if you ask me); Patrick, a tax accountant (a plain, old-fashioned bore); and Chris, a dental surgeon (drills, large needles, and pain).

I've changed a lot since then, even if my father hasn't. I've figured out that my parents probably aren't going to get back together. I understand that my mother likes Ted now. I know she deserves to be happy. And I know better than to tell my father anything.

"My lips are sealed," I told my mother. But I didn't add that just because I wasn't going to say anything to my father, it didn't mean that he was never going to find out. She already knew that.

My mother relaxed. "So," she said, "are the people at the animal shelter nice?"

.   .   .

"Can you meet me tomorrow after I get off work?" Billy said when he called after supper.

"Why?" I said. "What are you protesting now?"

Not only was Billy a dedicated animal rights activist, but he was spending the summer working at a social justice camp that got kids involved in all kinds of causes, from protecting the environment to fighting against child labor.

"Nothing," Billy said. "I swear. I still feel bad about what happened." I already knew that. He had called me twice over the weekend to apologize. "I want to make it up to you. I want to take you out to dinner and a movie."

A couple of "I'm sorry" phone calls I could understand. But dinner and a movie? That didn't sound like Billy.

"You've been talking to Morgan, haven't you?" I said. Morgan had been disappointed when I told her that I couldn't join her at her cottage as planned. She'd become furious when she found out the reason why: "Because of one of Billy's save-the-world protests? What about saving my summer?" Morgan's focus, unlike Billy's, was on her own species—and on one member of it in particular.

"I just want to do something nice for you, you know, because if it wasn't for me . . ."

"She yelled at you, didn't she, Billy?"

"Yeah," Billy said with a sigh. "She sort of said I ruined her summer—and yours."

"Sort of?"

"You know Morgan."

I did. She expressed her feelings freely. She dispensed advice even more freely.

"It's okay, Billy. You didn't ruin my summer, and I'm not mad at you."

"I still want to take you out, Robyn. *Please?*"

I know Billy as well as I know Morgan. Morgan had made him feel worse than he already did, and he would go right on feeling terrible until I let him do what Morgan wanted.

"Okay," I said. "Dinner and a movie sounds nice. Where do you want to go?"

"There's a vegan restaurant a couple of blocks from the camp. I can meet you there, if that's okay, and we can walk to the theater from there."

I told him that sounded great.

CHAPTER **FIVE**

My job: help the shelter's fund-raising committee by entering names and addresses into a database. Sitting next to my computer was a cardboard box filled with photocopies of checks, lists of participants at events such as the shelter's annual dog-walk-a-thon, and clip-out coupons from the shelter's newsletter or its calendar—which, by the way, featured cute and cuddly dogs, not fierce-looking dogs like Orion and the two pit bulls I had met the previous day. The mound of paper would have had my very organized mother delivering lectures on the perils of disorganization.

I pulled the first coupon out of the box, read the name and address written on it, checked both against a website Janet had showed me, and made a couple of corrections on the original piece of paper. Then I entered the information into the database. Even though I understood why all this checking was important—"Would you make a donation to an organization that couldn't even be bothered to spell your name correctly or get your address right?" Janet had said—I couldn't help thinking that a few days of this would have me begging the powers-that-be to open the schools early.

From where I sat, I had a good view of the shelter's two main wings, the heat-seared lawn between them, and the parking lot beyond. Every now and again I glanced out the window and saw shelter staff members taking the shortcut across the lawn from one wing to the other. By mid-morning, the volunteer dog walkers were outside with their charges. They were mostly retired people, according to Kathy. One of them in particular caught my eye—a thin old man with snow-white hair. He was working with a dog that looked an awful lot like Orion. I looked more closely. It *was* Orion—I was sure of it. *Good luck*, I thought, turning back to my computer. I checked and entered a few more names and addresses into the database, and then I glanced out the window again.

The old man had taken Orion into a fenced-in area of the yard. I watched them. The man didn't seem the least bit nervous. Nor did Orion seem the least bit fierce. He was sitting, but his ears stood at attention. He seemed utterly focused on the man, who was standing beside him, facing him. The man curled his hand into a fist, as if he were hiding something in it. He held the hand in front of Orion's nose for a moment. Then, slowly, the man pivoted around so that he was facing in the same direction as Orion. He squatted down and lowered his hand from Orion's nose, past his chest, and down to the ground. Orion remained sitting—which I found astonishing—and lowered his head to follow the old man's fist. The man swept his fist along the ground farther away from Orion. The dog slid forward to get closer to it until finally he was lying down. I saw the old man smile. He brought his hand to Orion's mouth and opened it. Orion gobbled something out of it. The man clapped his hands, and Orion stood up. Then the man got him to sit. He ran through the whole sequence with Orion again. He was training the dog, I realized. He seemed pretty good at it too, which made me wonder if he were really a staff member, not a volunteer.

"Not again," I heard someone exclaim. Kathy bustled past my door. She did not look happy. When I turned to the window, I saw her marching across the lawn toward the old man and the big dog. Her expression was serious as she talked to the man. The old man shook his head. Kathy said something else. The old man didn't look any happier than Kathy, but he finally nodded. The next thing I knew, he was leading Orion back to the animal wing. *What was that all about?* I wondered.

. . .

The shelter was air-conditioned, for which I was grateful. August was turning out to be even hotter than July had been. Not only had the grass withered from green to brown, but the leaves were curling on the few trees on the property. It hadn't rained for weeks. But as hot as it was, I couldn't stand staying indoors all day. I like to breathe real air, not climate-controlled air, as often as possible. There was a picnic table at one side of the yard, shaded by a large umbrella. At lunchtime I peeked out at it and saw that it was empty. I collected my sandwich and juice from the staff fridge and headed for the table.

By the time I got there, someone else had claimed a space. The old man who had been working with Orion was sitting at one end of the table. There was a thermos in front of him. I hesitated. Did I really want to spend my lunch break talking to an old guy I didn't know? I glanced around but didn't see any other shady spots. The man noticed me and smiled.

"Don't tell me one of you people has decided to brave the elements," he said. He waved me over. "Come on. I don't bite." He laughed—animal shelter humor, I guess—and stood up when I reached the table. He reminded me of my grandfather—my father's father, who was in a nursing home in New York State. Grandpa Hunter always leaped to his feet when a "lady" approached, just like this man was doing. If the bench hadn't been attached to the table, he probably would have pulled it out for me, just like Grandpa Hunter.

"Mort Schuster," the old man said, catching one of my hands in a grip of iron and pumping it.

"Robyn Hunter," I said, sitting on the bench opposite him.

"Pleased to meet you, Robyn," Mr. Schuster said. He sat down again, unscrewed the lid of his thermos, and poured something into a cup.

"Hot tea?" I said.

Mr. Schuster grinned. "A hot beverage actually cools you down on a day like this," he said. "Of course, it doesn't work the other way around." He peered across the table at me while he sipped his tea. "You look pretty young to be working here full-time. Summer job?" he said.

"Something like that," I said. "What about you? I saw you with one of the dogs this morning. Do you work here?"

"I certainly do," he said. "Five days a week for the past six years. But I don't get paid for it. I'm a volunteer."

"You must really like animals," I said, impressed. "Do you have a dog of your own?"

He shook his head. "I'm between animals, as they say. Jinx passed away a couple of months ago. He was eighteen years old." He shook his head. "I should be lucky enough to live that long."

I had to do some quick math in my head to work out that eighteen dog years was the equivalent of 85 years. I wasn't sure that I would ever want to be that old.

"I've always had a dog," Mr. Schuster said. "Always liked their company. It got to be even more important after I retired and my wife died."

"I'm sorry," I murmured.

He smiled at me. "I'm thinking of adopting," he said. "There are plenty of fine animals here that haven't had it so good. That dog I was working with this morning, he's like a big unruly kid, always seeing what he can get away with. But there's a good chance he can be broken of his bad habits." He glanced back at the building, in the general direction of Kathy's office. "He needs a lot more work, though," he said. "It takes six to eight weeks to break a dog of undesirable behavior, and three to four weeks to lock in a new behavior. But who knows? Maybe he'll be the one for me—*if* they get sensible around here and let someone with experience work with him." I had the feeling he was referring to his conversation with Kathy this morning. But it was really none of my business, so I didn't ask. Mr. Schuster peered more closely at me.

"Don't tell me, let me guess—you're not a dog person," he said. "Cats more to your liking?"

"Actually, I'm allergic to cats." After five minutes of direct exposure to a cat, I start to sneeze. After ten minutes, my eyes begin to water. After fifteen minutes, they turn red and itch so badly that I feel like scratching them out of my head.

Mr. Schuster opened his mouth to speak but was stopped by a whoop of laughter. I looked around and saw a gang of boys swarming out of the parking lot and onto the lawn. At first it looked as if they were headed our way. Then one of them pointed in our direction and the whole group ground to a halt. They conferred for a few moments before changing direction. One of them—Nick—glanced back over his shoulder at me. He was frowning. I watched them disappear inside the building.

"Good riddance," Mr. Schuster said.

"Who are they?" I said.

"In my day we called them juvenile delinquents." I looked from his bitter face to the door through which Nick and his friends had just disappeared.

"They can't be that bad if they're volunteering here," I said.

"*Volunteering?*" Mr. Schuster said, his contempt deepening. "They aren't volunteering. They're here because they *have* to be here." He shook his head. "Young offenders, that's what they call them these days. Future convicts is what they really mean."

I thought about Nick and what I already knew about him.

"Kids like that don't know the first thing about volunteering," Mr. Schuster said. "You have to be capable of thinking about someone besides yourself. The only thing those kids think about is themselves. They're always looking for a way to get something for nothing. That's what got them in trouble in the first place." His anger stunned me. "I'm sorry," he said, reading my expression. "I know I'm ranting. I just can't help myself. Kids like those really get me going. If I were in charge, I wouldn't let those violent criminals within a mile of this place."

"Violent?" I said.

"Every single one of those young fellows has been in trouble with the law," Mr. Schuster said. "And I don't mean jaywalking or stealing a pack of gum from the corner store. I mean serious trouble. The reason they're here is that they've been charged with at least one violent crime. And now some weak-kneed do-gooder has decided that working with animals is just the cure for their violent tendencies." He snorted.

"Violent crime?" I said. "What kind of violent crime?"

"We're not allowed to know that," Mr. Schuster said. "Those young fellows could go out and kill someone, and we wouldn't be allowed to know. *They're* protected by the law."

I know from my mother, who sometimes works with young offenders, that it's illegal to report their names in the media. Mr. Schuster swallowed the last of his tea and screwed the top back onto his thermos. He snapped the lid onto the plastic container that had held his lunch. "Well, work doesn't do itself," he said as he stood up. "It was very nice to meet you, Robyn."

Before I could ask him how working with dogs could cure Nick—or anyone else, for that matter—of violent tendencies, he was striding away from the picnic table. For an old guy, he sure moved fast.

.   .   .

I had to transfer buses twice to get all the way from the animal shelter to the vegan restaurant near where

Billy worked. Billy was waiting for me outside. He's tall and thin and knows more about animals than anyone I've ever met. He's planning to be a wildlife biologist.

"You really didn't have to do this," I told him again as we sat down.

"I hope you'll like this place, Robyn."

"If you like it, I know I will," I said.

In fact, the menu looked great. It was amazing how creative vegans could be in coming up with dishes that came 100 from the plant world—no meat, no cheese, no eggs, nothing that came from animals.

We ordered and Billy started to tell me about a project he was working on with some of the camp kids. They'd drawn up a petition to ask the city for permission to paint a mural on a pedestrian walkway that was covered in graffiti.

"They've done studies," Billy said. "Murals are a good way to combat graffiti. Graffiti artists respect other artists. Murals also beautify a neighborhood, *and* if they're well done, they can even educate people. We want to do ours on—"

Suddenly his eyes skipped from my face to somewhere over my shoulder. He shrank a little in his seat. I turned around to see what the problem was.

Terrific.

I looked back at Billy.

"Of all the people who had to walk in here, it had to be him," I said. "Don't look. Maybe he won't notice us."

No such luck.

Behind me Evan Wilson called, "Hey, Billy. There you are."

There you are? It sounded almost as if Evan had come in looking for Billy.

"Tell me this is a coincidence," I said under my breath. "Tell me you didn't plan this."

"I didn't. Honest," Billy said. He looked miserable.

"He isn't coming over here, is he, Billy?" I said. *"Please* tell me he isn't coming over here."

Billy sank lower in his seat.

A hand fell on my shoulder.

"Robyn," Evan said, giving me a little squeeze. "Good to see you again."

I glowered at Billy, who shook his head and mouthed the word, "Honest."

"Hey, Robyn, what you did at that protest was awesome," Evan said. He dropped into the empty chair beside me.

"That was an accident," I said. The sooner he found out that I was not the earnest, dedicated activist that he thought I was, the sooner he'd (maybe) leave me alone.

"Yeah, well, it was still awesome. Because of what you did, we got news coverage—print *and* TV."

Things just kept getting better.

"But they didn't show your picture, Robyn," Billy said quickly. "They didn't even mention your name. They just said there was a scuffle."

"So, Robyn," Evan said, grinning and leaning to-ward me. "Now that you're so into protesting, I was wondering—"

I stood up.

"I just remembered I'm low on cash," I said.

"But this is supposed to be my tr—"

I silenced Billy with a sharp look.

"I have to run out to the ATM," I said. "I won't be long." As I circled the table, I bent and whispered into Billy's ear: "Make him go away." I headed for the door. Before I pushed it open and stepped outside, I glanced back at the table. Billy was looking forlornly at me. I ignored him. My plan: I would give Billy five minutes to get rid of Evan. If he hadn't done the job by the time I returned, well, then I would just have to do my very best Morgan impression and get rid of him myself.

There was a cash machine two blocks from the res-taurant, near the bus stop. I'd spotted it when I arrived and had been planning to hit it before we went to the movies—I really was low on cash. I headed for it and took out some money. I was waiting to cross the street on my way back to the restaurant when a bus pulled up. Its doors opened, and a young woman struggled down the rear steps with a brand-new stroller heaped high with colorful bags and boxes. A bouquet of balloons was tied with ribbon to the handle of the stroller. Baby shower, I guessed.

One of the stroller wheels got wedged in the bus door, and the young woman looked flustered as she tried to work it free. I hurried over to give her a hand. She was wearing a waitress uniform from a chain restaurant and a name tag that said *Angie*.

"Thank you," she said when we had finally freed the stroller. Her face was flushed, and her round belly strained at the fabric of her uniform.

"Do you need help with that?" I asked.

She shook her head. "I'm fine," she said. "I live right there." She gestured to an apartment building almost directly opposite the vegan restaurant. "But thanks, anyway." Suddenly her face brightened, and she raised an arm and waved. She pushed her over-burdened stroller toward a guy with rust-colored hair who was about to enter the apartment building. He turned and started toward her. As I crossed the street, I heard her say, "Did you get the job?"

The bad news: when I got back to the restaurant, Evan was still there. The good news: he stood up as soon as I sat down.

"I'd better run," he said. "Nothing worse than being a third wheel, right, Billy?" He winked at Billy and flashed him a big grin.

I watched Evan walk out of the restaurant. "What just happened?" I said.

Billy shrugged and looked down at the tablecloth.

"Evan didn't come here because of me, did he, Billy? Because I told you yesterday that I wasn't interested in going out with him."

"And I told him that," Billy said. "He called me right after I talked to you."

"And you said, 'Robyn's not interested in you, Evan'—those were your exact words?"

Billy squirmed. "I think I might have said you were maybe interested in someone else—you know, so he wouldn't keep pestering me about it. But I didn't go into details," he added quickly. "I didn't think it was any of his business."

"Not to mention that it's not true," I said.

Billy's cheeks turned pink.

"It sounded to me like Evan knew you were going to be here today," I said.

"Yeah," Billy said. He looked around, as if he wished our food would hurry up and arrive.

"You told him, didn't you?"

"We were just talking, you know, the way you talk to the people you work with." He was slumped in his chair again. "I guess he just decided to take a shot."

"Even though you told him I was interested in someone else." Which I wasn't.

"Well, you know Evan."

I did. He was self-righteous and overly zealous, bordering on dogmatic. Apparently, he was also arrogant enough to think he could win me away from my (non-existent) boyfriend. I looked across the table at Billy. There was something else going on.

"He mentioned a third wheel," I said. "And he winked at you, Billy."

"What?"

"Evan. He winked at you."

"He did? I didn't notice."

Billy is many things, but a good liar isn't one of them.

"What exactly did you say to make him leave, Billy?"

"Ah, um . . ." Billy looked down at the tablecloth again. "I might have told him a sort of white lie," he said.

"Sort of, huh?" I watched Billy squirm some more. "Such as?"

"I might have given him the impression that maybe we were here together because you were maybe interested in . . ." His voice faded away.

"Say that again, Billy."

"Me," Billy said in a whisper. "It's possible that Evan has the impression that you're interested in me." He dared a glance at me. "I just wanted to get rid of him like you said, Robyn. I'd never be even remotely interested in you."

Of course not.

"Not in a million years," he said, for emphasis. "I mean, why would I be?"

Why indeed?

"Thanks, Billy," I said.

Thanks a lot.

. . .

I was in the staff kitchen at the animal shelter the next day, when Nick walked in. He waited until I was finished taking my lunch out of the fridge before getting his. At least, I assumed it was his lunch. It was in a brown paper bag.

I went outside. I had planned to sit at the picnic table and read while I ate. Nick was right behind me. About three feet from the table, we both realized that we were headed for the same place, and we stopped. He looked at me and then stepped back a pace.

"It's okay," he said. "You can have it."

"No, you go ahead," I said. "You and your friends have been here longer than I have."

"They're not here today," he said.

"Oh."

We stared at each other. I knew who he was, but he obviously hadn't recognized me. I wanted to keep it that way.

He looked from me to the picnic table and back again. "It's a big table," he said. "You've got a book. I've got a book." He nodded at the backpack slung over one shoulder. "I'm quiet when I read. I don't even move my lips," he said.

He seemed nice. I think that's what threw me. I knew what he had done a few years back. I also knew from what Mr. Schuster had told me, that he hadn't changed much. But he seemed nice, and his purple-blue eyes sparkled the way my father's gray eyes did when he was in a particularly good mood.

"Okay," I said.

We sat down. I unwrapped my sandwich, took the lid off my juice, and opened my book. He tipped out his lunch bag—a sandwich, an orange, some cookies and . . . dog biscuits. Two big ones wrapped in plastic. He grabbed them, shoved them into his backpack, and looked across the table at me with a guilty expression on his face.

"They're homemade," he said.

"You make *dog* biscuits?" I couldn't picture it.

He shook his head. "Not me. There's this bakery that I know that does. The biscuits are kind of expensive, but they're all natural and Orion likes them." He glanced back at the office building. "Don't tell, okay?"

I didn't say anything. He pulled a book from his backpack—a thick, hard-covered book about dogs. I peeked at the cover as he opened it. He had printed his name on the inside front cover in big black letters. Something else was written under that, but I couldn't make out what it was. He also took out a yellow highlighter. Before he started reading, he looked at me again.

"I know I already asked you this," he said, "but are you sure we haven't met before? You look kind of familiar."

I didn't hesitate. "No," I said. "I would have remembered."

He grinned in surprise.

"Really?" he said.

I felt my cheeks burn.

"What I mean is—" I began.

"That's okay," he said, amused at my discomfort. "I know what you mean. I think I would have remembered too."

For a while, we read and ate in silence. Then—I'm not sure how—we started talking. Nick was telling me what he had learned about dogs and especially what he had learned about Orion.

"Dogs are really smart," he said. "People didn't used to think so, but they've done all kinds of studies. This one guy, he wanted to see if dogs could count. So he took five meatballs and put them in one spot on the ground, and then he put just one meatball in another spot. Then he studied which meatballs the dogs would go to first. Guess what they picked, every time."

I had no idea.

"The closest ones," Nick said. "They went for whatever was closest, whether it was five meatballs or just one. *Except*," he said, "when the five meatballs and the one meatball were the same distance from the dogs. Then they went for the five meatballs. Proving—"

"That to dogs, good food means whatever food they can get to quickest," I said. "Kind of a whole new definition of fast food."

Nick laughed. If I hadn't known him from before and didn't know why he was here now, my overall impression would have been that he had a future as a vet or a kennel owner. He really loved dogs. He glowed when he talked about Orion.

"My plan," he said, "is to adopt Orion."

I opened my mouth to tell him that Mr. Schuster had the same plan. Then I clamped it shut again and told myself that it was none of my business. Although I enjoyed talking to him, I was glad when my break was over and I had an excuse to leave. He didn't know who I was. With any luck, he wouldn't remember.

I ran into him again later in the day. I was on my way back from the kitchen with a glass of ice water when I heard a voice from inside my cubbyhole of an office.

"I told you, I'll get it," the voice was saying. I peeked inside. It was Nick. He was using my phone. "Relax, Joey," he said. "It's gonna be okay. I'll figure something out and I'll get back to you." Silence. "Tell her it's going to be okay," he said. "There's no way I'd let that happen." Another long pause. "It won't be long before you're driving again. Then it'll all be good. You tell her I said so . . . . Yeah. Look, Joey, I gotta go."

He hung up the phone and turned around. I could tell he was startled to see me standing there. He stared at me as if waiting for me to explain why I had been eavesdropping on his conversation.

"You're in my office," I said.

He looked even more surprised. "Sorry," he said. "I had to make a call." He glanced around. "Is there any way you could maybe not mention this to anyone?" he said.

I shrugged. It was just a phone call. What was there to mention?

He brushed past me, strode down the hall, and pushed open an exterior door. A little later when I looked out the window, I saw him on the grass with Orion, putting him through his paces. He seemed as relaxed out there with the big dog as he had been at lunch. He sure didn't look like the violent criminal that Mr. Schuster seemed to hold in such disdain.

. . .

Toward the end of the next day, Kathy stuck her head into my office. "Need a break?" she said.

I didn't want to appear overly eager to stop, but you can only stare at a computer screen for so long before you crave a change of scenery. I nodded.

"One of our volunteer committees is meeting in about half an hour," she said, "and we're shorthanded. Would you mind helping Janet set up?"

"No problem."

She told me where to find Janet. "The quickest way," she said, "is to go out that door." She pointed down the hall. "Then cut across to the adoption center." The adoption center was located near the parking lot.

I followed her directions and reached the parking lot just as a van pulled to a stop and its driver tooted the horn. Nick and his friends surged toward it from a patch of shade where they had been waiting. I glanced at Nick. He was looking at me, but there was nothing friendly about his expression. I ducked my head and tried to skirt the group, unnoticed, but Nick planted himself in my path.

"Hey," he said. "It's been bugging me since the first day, but now I know who you are." His purple-blue eyes were as hard as amethyst. "You're the girl who turned me in."

CHAPTER SIX

"Aren't you going to deny it?" he said.

He was standing so close to me that I could feel his breath on my face. I stepped back. He was a lot bigger than he had been when I knew him before, back when I was in junior high. He looked a lot stronger now too. He was staring at me so ferociously that I shifted my eyes down to the ground, just like I would have done if he were a dog. But he wasn't a dog, I told myself. He was just a guy. Yes, he was taller than me. Yes, he looked like he could do some serious damage if he wanted to. And yes, I wanted nothing more than to get away from him. But if I fled, he would think I was afraid of him. There was no way I was going to give him that satisfaction. Besides, I hadn't done anything wrong. In fact, just the opposite.

I looked up and met his eyes.

"Why would I deny it?" I said. "I just did what any normal person would have done if they'd been in my place."

He nodded as if I'd said pretty much what he had expected.

"You recognized me, didn't you?" he said. His eyes were drilling into me. He seemed to be daring me to answer.

"So what if I did?"

The driver of the van looked in our direction. She was an older woman, dressed in jeans and a T-shirt, with a pair of sunglasses shoved up on top of her head. She was passing out boxes of juice to the rest of the boys, who crowded around the van. When she finished, she looked over at us, reached into the van, and tooted the horn.

"Come on, Nick!" she called. "This train is about to leave the station."

But Nick didn't head for the van. Instead, he leaned forward, trying to intimidate me.

"You don't scare me," I said.

"Is that right?" He stepped closer. I fought the urge to retreat a pace. "Then how come you pretended you didn't know me?"

"Nick!" The woman tooted the horn again. Only then did Nick tear his eyes from me. He adjusted the backpack that hung from one of his shoulders, wheeled around and marched toward the van. I turned and slipped into the cool of the building in front of me.

. . .

The next afternoon, I looked up from my computer and saw Nick and the other guys outside with their dogs.

"If I were your age, I'd be sneaking a peek too," a voice behind me said.

I spun around, my face flushed, feeling like I'd been caught staring out the window at school when I should have been paying attention to the teacher. Kathy stood in the doorway to my office, smiling.

"Some of those guys are really cute, aren't they?" she said.

I glanced outside again. When Kathy was my age, she must have gone for the bad-boy type.

"I heard that they've all been in trouble with the law," I said.

Kathy looked surprised. "Who told you that?"

"Mr. Schuster," I said. "He told me that they have to be here because they've all been charged with violent crimes."

Kathy looked around for a chair, but I was sitting on the only one in the room. She leaned against the wall instead.

"He really shouldn't have said anything," she said. "But since he did, it is true that all of the participants of the RAD program have been mandated by the court to take anger management counseling."

"RAD?" I said.

"Rehabilitate A Dog," she said. "But the kids who participate in RAD don't have to be here. They all had a choice. They could have attended a traditional anger management program, one day a week for eight weeks. Or they could come here four days a week for eight weeks. RAD is a much bigger commitment, but these kids chose it because they thought it would be more interesting to work with dogs."

"Mr. Schuster seems to think it's crazy to trust them with the dogs," I said. I thought about how Nick had tried to intimidate me the day before and decided that I didn't entirely disagree with him.

Kathy shook her head. "They're young. They can change. And the program works. We teach participants how to work with the dogs to modify their behavior. All the dogs in the program have been abandoned by their owners. They have . . ." She paused and groped for words. "Let's just say that they're very challenging dogs," she said.

"Challenging?" I thought about my encounter with Orion. He had tried to scare me, just like Nick had. He'd even charged me. "You mean, they're vicious?" I said.

"No," Kathy said. "Not vicious."

"Have any of them attacked people?" I said.

She looked directly at me. "Bitten, yes. Attacked, no."

I wasn't sure I saw the difference.

"Some dogs are really aggressive," Kathy said. "You've probably read about dog attacks in the newspaper from time to time—a dog mauls a child or attacks and kills another dog. Sometimes we get animals like that. Sometimes we have to put them down."

"But these dogs aren't like that?"

She shook her head again.

"The dogs in the RAD program have behavior problems that have made them unsuitable for adoption," she said. "Most of them were never trained properly. Their owners may have disciplined them by hitting them with a rolled-up newspaper or some other object."

The very idea seemed to exasperate her. "That's usually counterproductive. Instead of teaching the dog to behave, it teaches the dog that a hand coming toward it means punishment. It sees a hand reach out, and it bites. The dog owner may see that as an attack, but to the dog, it's self-defense. We have one dog in the program that was bought as a puppy. The owner kept the dog in the house when it was little and cute but never bothered to train it properly. Because the dog was never trained, when it got bigger, it started jumping up on people and making a nuisance of itself—and ended up getting punished by the owner. Finally, the owner chained it out in his backyard. The dog spent two years out there. It was never let off the chain and never let inside.

"Dogs are pack animals," she said. "They're very social. They need to be around other creatures—dogs, human beings, it doesn't matter. Imagine how you'd be if you were chained out in a yard all by yourself, winter and summer, night and day, for two years. Someone finally reported the owner. We seized the dog. If we can rehabilitate him, he has a chance to be adopted. If we can't . . ." She sighed. "Do you know what the leading cause of death is for dogs?"

The first thing that came to mind was getting hit by a car. But I guessed that probably wasn't the answer she was looking for. I shook my head.

"The leading cause of death for dogs is unwelcome behavior," Kathy said.

It took me a moment to digest this. "You mean, because the dog ends up being put down?"

She nodded. "That's what we're trying to avoid with the RAD program," she said. "It's kind of a last chance program for these dogs. The kids each take responsibility for a dog. It's up to them to work with the dogs to modify their behavior. At the same time, the program helps the kids. They learn that they can't get the behavior they want by yelling at their dogs or trying to bully them. They have to stay calm. They have to be patient. By the end of the program, the kids have learned a lot about how to control their own anger. And if we're lucky, most of the dogs are ready for adoption."

"*Most?*" I said.

"With consistent training and lots of positive reinforcement, most dogs succeed," she said.

"And the ones that don't?"

"If we can't find a home for an animal, well, eventually we run out of options."

Oh. I glanced out the window again. Nick and the others, together with their dogs, were all heading back across the field toward a man and a woman. I had seen the man before—he was the stocky guy with the brush-cut hair who had called to Nick the first day I was at the shelter. I didn't recognize the woman.

. . .

For my break that afternoon I took a bottle of juice and a book from my bag, and went to sit at the picnic table to read. I had only been outside for a couple of minutes when the kids from the RAD program spilled out onto the field near the parking lot for their break. It wasn't long before a Frisbee sailed through the air. One of the RAD participants raised his arm up, up, up and caught it. Then his arm arced back and he released the Frisbee again. It soared across the field to another RAD participant, who leaped clear off the ground to make the catch.

Nick was standing closest to the wing where the animals were kept. Someone threw the Frisbee in his direction. Nick moved toward it, looking up, gauging its distance. But the Frisbee was too close and still too high. Nick reversed direction, running backward now, looking up, his eyes focused on the blue disc.

As Nick ran backward, Mr. Schuster appeared around the side of the animal building leading a small dog on a leash. He was headed for the door to go inside. His attention was focused on the dog, which was balking. Mr. Schuster bent down to say something to the dog or to coax it along. I don't think he saw Nick. I know Nick didn't see Mr. Schuster. The rest of the RAD guys did, though. They saw what I saw—Nick running backward, his gaze directed up at the Frisbee, his hand swinging up now, moving to make a grab for it. But they all just stood there, watching, as the gap between Nick and Mr. Schuster got smaller and smaller until . . .

"Mr. Schuster!" I shouted. "Mr. Schuster, look out!"

Mr. Schuster turned to see Nick bearing down on him, but it was too late. Nick slammed into him. Mr. Schuster flew sideways. The little dog scrambled out of the way and narrowly missed being squashed when Mr. Schuster hit the ground. Nick lost his balance on impact and fell on top of the old man. Everyone, including me, ran toward them.

Nick had sprung to his feet by the time I reached Mr. Schuster. He was leaning over the old man, his hand outstretched. Mr. Schuster struggled into a sitting position. His face was pale. He slapped Nick's hand away.

"Thug," he said.

Nick's face clouded.

The door to the animal building opened, and Kathy came out. She took in the situation. "What happened?" she said to the RAD guys.

"He fell," one of them said.

"Fell?" Mr. Schuster spluttered. He was rubbing one shoulder. "That young hooligan knocked me off my feet and threw himself on top of me," he said. He glared at Nick. "You should keep those kids on a leash!"

"Hey!" Nick said. His eyes blazed. He started toward the old man. One of the other RAD guys grabbed him by the arm and pulled him back.

"It's not worth it," the guy said.

"It was an accident," Nick said.

"There are no such things as accidents," Mr. Schuster said. "There are only preventable injuries. If you'd been watching where you were going, it never would have happened."

"Yeah, well—" Nick began. Kathy looked at him, her brown eyes signaling a warning. Nick shut his mouth and kicked the Frisbee, which had landed near his feet. It scudded across the grass.

Kathy turned back to Mr. Schuster. "Let me help you up," she said.

Mr. Schuster didn't push her away as he had pushed away Nick. Kathy strained with the effort of hoisting the old man to his feet. I rushed forward to help.

"Are you all right, Mort?" Kathy said. "Are you hurt?"

Mr. Schuster leaned heavily on us. He seemed to be dragging one leg.

"Let's help him to the picnic table," Kathy said to me. "You can catch your breath there, okay, Mort?"

The old man grunted. "The dog," he said.

I glanced back over my shoulder at the little dog Mr. Schuster had been walking. The poor thing was cowering near a bush.

"Dougie," Kathy said to one of the RAD participants. "Take the dog inside."

A hulking guy with a skull tattooed on his left forearm picked up the leash and yanked on it.

"Gently, for Pete's sake," Mr. Schuster said. "That's an animal, not a wagon."

Dougie shot a sour look at Mr. Schuster. Then he looked down at the dog. "Come on," he said to the dog, guiding it more gently now.

Mr. Schuster limped all the way to the picnic table. I don't think he would have made it if we hadn't been helping him. By the time he dropped down onto the bench, he was breathing heavily.

"Do you want me to run you over to the hospital?" Kathy said. "Maybe it would be a good idea to have a doctor take a look at you."

"Maybe you should run those troublemakers to the county lockup," Mr. Schuster said.

Kathy's lips tightened. Out in the field, Nick's arms were flying in all directions as he talked to the rest of the RAD participants. He looked upset. The door to the animal wing opened again, and the man with the brush-cut hair came out with Dougie. He walked directly to Nick, whose hands flew around even more wildly while he presumably explained what had happened. The man with the brush-cut hair, who reminded me of a drill sergeant in a war movie, said something. I saw Nick shake his head—no, no, no. Then the man said something that made Nick go rigid. The rest of the guys, who had been standing around listening, pressed in a little closer. Nick shook his head again. He seemed more subdued now. The man said something else.

Finally, Nick wheeled away from the group and started across the field. His hands were clenched into fists at his sides. The man with the brush-cut hair followed a few paces behind.

Nick came to a stop in front of the picnic table. He looked down at Mr. Schuster, who was massaging the leg that had been dragging. Mr. Schuster glowered at him.

"I'm sorry," Nick said. But he didn't sound sorry. He sounded resentful. "I didn't see you. I hope you're okay."

"No thanks to you," Mr. Schuster said.

I saw anger rise in Nick the way mercury rises in a thermometer on a hot day. The man with the brush-cut hair laid a hand on Nick's arm.

"Back to the group, D'Angelo," he said. "Now."

Nick spun around and scowled at the man. He didn't say anything. After a moment, he stalked back across the field to the rest of the group.

"It really was an accident, Mr. Schuster," I said.

"Punk kid," Mr. Schuster muttered. "Did you hear him? He sounded like he was going to choke on that apology."

He was right. Nick had sounded anything but apologetic. If I had knocked Mr. Schuster over, I couldn't have apologized fast enough. But then, if I had knocked Mr. Schuster over, he wouldn't have treated me the way he'd treated Nick. I glanced across the field and saw a sullen-faced Nick filing back inside with the rest of the RAD guys.

CHAPTER **SEVEN**

I was in my office the following Monday, checking and double-checking names and addresses, when I heard someone yelling outside. I looked out the window and saw Kathy standing beside her little red Firefly, which she had pulled up to the back entrance of the office wing. The trunk of the car was open, and she was waving to the man with the brush-cut hair. I'd learned that his name was Ed Jarvis. He was the youth counselor responsible for the kids in the RAD program. The RAD kids were out in the field with their dogs. The first thing they did every day when they arrived at the shelter was to take their dogs outside for ten minutes before they reported to their training sessions.

Mr. Jarvis walked over to Kathy's car, and he and Kathy exchanged words. Then he called out to the boys. Nick and two of his friends handed their dogs' leashes to the other RAD participants and jogged over to join Kathy and Mr. Jarvis. Mr. Jarvis spoke to them. Nick and the other two boys reached into the trunk of Kathy's car. Each hoisted out a cardboard box. I was baffled by the expressions on their faces. The boxes weren't very big, but all three boys seemed to be struggling with them. A few moments later, all three filed through the back door and carried their loads into the office directly across from mine.

"You can just set them down here," Kathy said before poking her head into my office. "Why don't you take a break from that for a few minutes, Robyn? I could use your help over here."

I followed her into the office across the hall.

Thud, thud, thud went the boxes as the three boys dropped them onto the desk.

"Man, what's in these, anyway?" one of them asked. "Lead?"

"Money," Kathy said.

"Must be *a lot* of money," the other boy said.

"It's mostly coins," Kathy said. "Dimes, nickels, quarters. But there are bills too. Fives, tens, twenties."

The first boy stared at the boxes as if he were trying to see through the cardboard. The second boy whistled softly.

"How much do you think is in there?" the first boy said.

"I'll let you know after it's been counted, Antoine," Kathy said.

"Want some help with that?" Antoine said. He looked hungrily at the boxes.

"Yeah, we'll count it for you," the other boy said. He sounded as eager as Antoine.

Of the three of them, only Nick didn't seem interested. The boxes might as well have been cement blocks as far as he was concerned.

Kathy laughed. "Thanks, but I think I can handle it," she said. "Besides, you guys are going to be late for class if you don't get a move on, and you know how Ed feels about tardiness."

Antoine and the other boy grumbled. Nick nudged Antoine, and the three of them trooped out of the office. Kathy grabbed a pair of scissors and cut the tape that sealed the boxes. All three were crammed with money. Just as Kathy had said, most of it was coins. But not all of it. There were plenty of bills—fives, ten, and twenties—peeking out from among the coins.

"It looks like someone just dumped everything in there," I said.

"That's exactly what happened," Kathy said. "We did campaigns at a couple of malls over the weekend—displays on animal cruelty, pictures of the animals we have for adoption, that kind of thing. We do mall displays at least once a month, when we can get enough volunteers together to set up and to stay to answer questions. We always have a container near the display to collect donations. They're big plastic balls, like the kind you see people using to collect donations around Christmas. People drop in their spare change. Some people are more generous and put in five or ten or even twenty dollars. At the end of the day, the containers get emptied into those reinforced boxes. I usually pick them up from the volunteer in charge on my way in on Monday." She looked down at the three boxes. "Now comes the fun part."

"Fun part?"

"I have some volunteers coming in later to roll the coins. We'll count it all then. But it would be nice to have things organized for them. Would you mind sorting out the coins, Robyn?"

"No problem," I said.

Kathy left me to the task. A moment later, I heard her voice in the hallway just outside the office door.

"Nick, what are you still doing here?" she said.

"I wanted to ask you something," Nick said.

"Well, it'll have to wait. You're already late. Now scoot!"

I pushed two of the boxes to the far end of the desk— it was like trying to shift a pile of bricks. Then I scooped handfuls of coins out of the third box until the box was light enough to tip out. I started by picking out all the paper money—there was even one fifty-dollar bill—and stacking it in piles, which I set at the back of the desk. Next, I sorted the coins. By the time I'd finished, I had a mound of each type of coin.

I emptied the second box onto the desk and went through the same process. The mounds grew into mountains. The stacks of paper money got higher too.

I had almost finished with the third box when I heard a shout—a scream?—from outside. Kathy thundered down the hallway past the office where I was working. I scurried across the hall to my own office and looked out the window.

Something was going on in the field outside. Kids, adults, and dogs were milling around, but I couldn't see what all the excitement was about. Then I heard another shout, loud and urgent. Someone banged on my window—Kathy, red-faced from running in the afternoon heat.

"911," she shouted. "Call 911. It's Mr. Schuster. Tell them he's breathing, but he's unconscious. He doesn't respond to my voice."

Unconscious?

I scrabbled for the phone and punched in the numbers. I was surprised at how calm my voice sounded while I told the 911 operator where I was calling from and what I was calling about. I told the operator Mr. Schuster's approximate age and repeated what Kathy had told me. Then I repeated the address of the shelter, reading it off the shelter calendar that hung on the wall near my computer. The whole time I was thinking, *Hang on, Mr. Schuster.*

After I hung up, I opened my window and called to let Kathy know that help was on the way. She nodded grimly. I was closing the window again when I heard a noise in the hall behind me. I started to turn. Out of the corner of my eye, I saw someone darting out of the office across the hall. At least, I thought that's what I saw. I wasn't positive. *Probably a staff member,* I thought. I turned to look out the window again. Then I couldn't stand it anymore. I had to find out how Mr. Schuster was.

I stepped out of my office, intending to go directly outside. Then—I'm not sure what made me do it—I glanced into the office where I had been sorting the money. The piles of coins looked more or less as I had left them, but the stacks of bills didn't. They had been knocked over. But what had scattered them?

Or who?

All the office doors were equipped with locks. You pressed a button on the inside door knob, pulled the door closed, and it locked automatically. You needed a key to open it again. I made sure to lock the money room. Then I went outside. I heard a siren in the distance—the 911-response unit. Nick and Antoine were standing just outside the building. But whereas everyone else was clustered on the field, surrounding Mr. Schuster, Nick and Antoine were just outside the back door, far away from the crowd. Antoine looked directly at me when I stepped out into the hot afternoon. His expression was not friendly. Nick looked at me too, but only for a moment, before ducking his head and turning away from me, all in one fluid motion. The two of them strode away across the lawn.

"Hey," I called to them. But the shrill of the siren drowned out my voice. An ambulance drove right out onto the field. Nick and Antoine disappeared behind it.

By the time I'd reached it, both boys had joined the rest of their group, and Mr. Jarvis was leading them off the field.

The paramedics got out of the ambulance and hurried over to Mr. Schuster. Kathy was kneeling beside him. Mr. Schuster's face was white, but his eyes were open now. A man with Kathy stood up and said something to the paramedics. I recognized him from the tour Kathy had given me on my first day—a vet. Relief flooding over Kathy's face as the paramedics took over. She squeezed one of Mr. Schuster's hands before moving out of their way.

"Is he going to be all right?" I said when she stepped away from him.

"I don't know," she said. She looked around at the staff members and volunteers who had gathered on the lawn. She started toward them, gently telling everyone to go back inside. "Mr. Schuster is in good hands," she said.

I hung back for a moment and looked across the lawn to Nick and the rest of the RAD group. They were all facing Mr. Jarvis. All except Nick. He was looking at me. Looking and not smiling. I wasn't smiling either. I was remembering something that had happened nearly four years ago. It was, as my father would have said, déjà vu all over again.

CHAPTER EIGHT

Four years ago, I attended an alternative junior high school called South Parkside Alternative—SPA, for short. The school was tiny: fifty kids in all, half in grade seven and half in grade eight, crammed into a couple of rooms on the top floor of a regular kindergarten-to-grade-eight school. There were always ten times more kids who wanted to go to SPA than there were places, so those of us who got in thought we were special. SPA was more fun than regular school. We went on more field trips and did more activities, which was great but made some kids in the regular school jealous. At SPA we were encouraged to not just study issues but to get involved—for extra credit, of course.

It was while I was at SPA that I became active in animal rights. Partly I was talked into it by Billy. Partly I was shamed into it by Morgan, who is one of life's positive thinkers and who believes that the best thing to do

71

when you fall off a horse is to climb right back on. While I wasn't about to shake paws with the dog that had bitten me, I was (eventually) willing to show no hard feelings by working to defend animal rights. And that's why Morgan, Billy, and I organized the pet pageant while we were at SPA—to raise money for Billy's favorite animal rights charity.

The pageant itself was the main event. We charged kids a dollar to enter their pets. We got pet supply stores and pet trainers in the area to donate items (little packages of dog and cat toys; baskets of dog, cat and hamster treats; and introductory dog training sessions) for prizes and a raffle. Two of the more artistic kids at SPA volunteered to do face painting—animal-themed, of course—for the little kids who attended. I let Morgan rope me into helping her with the cat race—which was pretty funny, because the cats didn't seem to understand or, more likely, care that they were supposed to be in a race. You know cats. After twenty minutes of trying to herd felines of all ages and sizes in the general direction of the finish line, my eyes were watering, my nose was running, and the audience, especially its younger members, was convulsed with laughter.

The pageant was a huge success and not just because school was let out early so that everyone could attend. We raised a lot of money.

At the end of the day, while the rest of the SPA kids were cleaning up, Billy, Morgan, and I took the money inside to be counted. We were going to give it to our teacher to deposit in the bank so that she could send a check to the animal rights group.

As we climbed the stairs to the top floor of the school, Morgan chattering away about how well everything had gone and Billy speculating about how much money we had raised (and probably wildly overestimating our results), I was still sneezing from exposure to the cats. SPA consisted of two large classrooms, a smaller room that served as a library, a multipurpose room where we held school meetings and ate lunch, and an office. Except for Morgan, Billy, and me, the school seemed deserted. Our teacher, Lois—we called all the teachers at SPA by their first names—said that she would come up after she had supervised the cleanup.

Morgan unlocked the office door with the key Lois had given her. We put the money—a couple of tin cans filled with coins and a fat envelope stuffed with bills—on Lois's desk. I pulled up a chair so that we could start counting. So did Morgan. Then Billy said he hadn't had a chance to eat anything all day, and Morgan, who is one of those skinny girls who is always munching, said that she'd been too busy to eat too. Since they'd mentioned it, I realized I was hungry too. So we decided to go back down and grab a bite to eat before we counted the money. We closed the office door, and I checked to make sure it was locked.

As we headed down the stairs to the school yard, I had a moment of panic. My keys! I was always losing them back then. My mother freaked out every time.

She's the kind of person who can't sleep at night unless she's already laid out her clothes for the next morning and has her briefcase packed and ready to go. Every time she had a new set of keys made for me, she attached them to a larger and bulkier key chain so that they would be harder to lose. The last key chain had a metal police whistle attached to it, and I had got into the habit of patting my pockets regularly to make sure it was still there. Usually it was. But that day, it was gone.

I sneezed. Then I got that frozen-up feeling that always came over me when I thought about admitting to my mother that my keys were missing—*again*. I'm usually the kind of person who tears the house apart looking for something when I lose it. When my father loses something, which he hardly ever does, he stands in one place, closes his eyes, and tries to visualize the last time he had held whatever it was in his hand. He won't open his eyes until he has that picture fixed in his mind. Then he goes directly to where he left whatever is missing. It's infuriating. But it works. That's what I tried that day.

I stopped on the stairs, gripped the railing, and closed my eyes. I heard Morgan, who was almost at the bottom, sigh and say, "Not again." She couldn't believe how often I misplaced my keys. Top of the class, she'd say. You skipped a grade, but you're completely scattered.

"I gave them back to you," I heard her say.

My eyes popped open. I looked at her and sneezed again.

"Just before we came inside," she said. "You gave them to me so I could use the whistle for the cat race. I gave them back to you when the race was over. Seriously, Robyn, anyone would think you *try* to lose your keys a couple of times a week. Maybe you're working out some issues with your mother. It's classic passive-aggressive behavior." Morgan's mother is a psychiatrist, so Morgan has always been hyperaware of people's behavior. She's always more than happy to provide her analysis too.

I closed my eyes again. This time I saw Morgan pressing my keys into my already full hands out in the schoolyard. I heard her saying, "Here. There's no way I'm going to take the blame if you lose them."

I had held the keys in my hand. They had dangled from my finger all the way up the stairs. I had put them down when I'd set down a couple of tin cans filled with coins and pulled a tissue from my back pocket to blow my nose again. I turned now and started up the stairs.

"Hey," Morgan called. She tossed me the key to the office door. "Meet you outside."

I scooted back up the stairs and pushed open the door at the top. That's when I heard voices—whispers—coming from the office. At first, I didn't think much about it. Maybe some other kids were putting things away. I turned the corner and saw that the door—the one I had just locked—was open now. I heard more whispering, frantic, like mice scurrying. I wasn't sure why, but it didn't sound right.

I sneezed.

Then I heard an urgent whisper: "Someone's coming."

Footsteps pounded toward me. Two boys exploded out of the office, almost bowling me over. One of them I sort of recognized—a short, dark-haired kid who went to the school where SPA was located. The other boy was a lot taller and a lot older. The younger kid paused when he saw me. The older kid barreled past me in a blur, grabbing the younger one on the way by. I heard a door crash against a cinder block wall and then footsteps fading down a flight of stairs. Shocked, I stepped into the office and looked around. The cans of coins were still there, but the envelope containing the bills was gone.

I spun around and looked at the door through which the two boys had disappeared. Then I sprinted down the stairs and out into the school yard. After a frantic few moments, I located Lois. I sped over to her and told her exactly what I had seen.

Based on my description, they caught the younger kid the next day, but I never heard anything about the older boy. And the money? We never got it back. Someone told me that the kid they'd caught said he'd acted alone. I knew that wasn't true. I told Lois and the school principal that there had been another boy with him. But because I had recognized the younger one, I had concentrated on him. I hadn't taken a good enough look at the other boy to be able to describe him. The kid I saw, the one I described first to Lois, and later to the police, was Nick D'Angelo. He was expelled from the school. I never saw him again—until now. Obviously, if he was participating in a program for kids who had been charged with violent crimes, things had gone from bad to worse for him.

. . .

I got Janet to unlock the door to the office across the hall from mine. I stood inside for five full minutes, maybe longer, trying to remember if I had bumped against the desk when I rushed out of the room. That would account for the knocked-over bills. But I hadn't. I was sure of it. And as far as I could tell, nothing else could have knocked or blown them over. No pictures or calendars had fallen off the wall. The window wasn't open. Nothing like that. But I *had* seen someone dart out of the office. Well, *sort of* seen someone. All I'd noticed was a flash of movement and the sound of footsteps. I'd told myself that it was just another staff member dashing down the hall. But if that were true, what had disturbed the piles of paper money that I had so carefully stacked? And why, when I'd gone to see what was happening, had Nick and Antoine been standing next to the door, far away from everyone else in their group? Nick and Antoine—two boys who were here because they had been in trouble before. Two boys who had helped carry in the money from Kathy's car and knew which office it was in. Antoine had been fascinated by how much money the boxes might contain.

Nick had lingered in the hallway long after Kathy had dismissed him. He'd said he wanted to talk to her. But had he really? Or had he been waiting to see what Kathy was going to do with the money?

I was thinking about what to do—what I *could* do, given that I wasn't even sure what had happened—when Kathy came back into the building. I asked her how Mr. Schuster was.

"I don't know yet," she said. "I'm going to call the hospital in a little while. I should have insisted on taking him there on Friday after his accident. I know he has a heart condition." She sighed. "He can be pretty stubborn, but he sure knows dogs. Loves them too."

"I saw him working with Orion last week," I said.

"Yes, well, that's another story," Kathy said. A story that she didn't go on to tell me. Someone called her from down the hall, and she excused herself.

After Kathy left, I kept thinking about the money. I finished sorting the coins into piles. I stacked the bills again and then stared at the stacks, trying to decide if they were the same size as they had been before or if they were smaller. I wasn't sure. Kathy returned with three women who all seemed to know one another well. After nodding at me, they pulled up some chairs, settled in and started rolling coins, chattering to one another the whole time.

I went back to my office and looked out the window. After the RAD group worked with their dogs, they usually took a break before reporting to another room in the shelter complex where they talked about what they had learned and, according to Kathy, how the lessons applied to their own lives. I waited until I saw Nick, Antoine, and the rest of the group come out of the animal wing and claim the picnic table.

By the time I approached them, the picnic table was littered with chip bags and candy wrappers. Three or four of the RAD guys were talking at the same time, each one shouting to be heard over the others. A couple of others were laughing. They reminded me of the gang of boys at my school who always held down the same table in the same corner of the cafeteria and always made more noise than everyone else combined. Guys who thought they were so cool. Guys who were overcompensating, according to Morgan.

I hesitated. Then I told myself that I was not the least bit intimidated by these boys, even though that wasn't, strictly speaking, true. I drew in a deep breath, just like I do when I have to get up in front of the whole class and do a presentation or—*shudder*—give a speech.

"Excuse me," I said. The words came out of my mouth at the exact moment that one of the guys said something uproariously funny—or so his buddies seemed to think. They all exploded in laughter. I waited until they settled down a little.

"Excuse me," I said again. This time I tapped Nick on the shoulder.

Every guy at the table turned to look at me. Every guy except Nick.

"Hello?" I said, tapping him harder this time, feeling the bone of his shoulder.

The guy sitting next to Nick nudged him and said something about me that made my cheeks turn red. He grinned up at me and then slowly licked his lips. I gave him the imperious, "just who do you think you are?" look that Morgan had perfected. Then I turned my attention to Nick.

"Can I speak with you for a minute?" I said.

He looked up at me.

"Go for it," he said.

"Alone," I said. "I'd like to talk to you alone."

This provoked a chorus from his friends: *"Oooooooh!"* They sounded like a bunch of kindergarten kids, but they leered at me like a pack of wolves. Dougie, who was sitting closest to Nick, slapped him on the back.

"All *right*, man," he said.

Nick didn't move. He just sat there, maybe looking at the can of Coke in front him, maybe looking at the tabletop, maybe just looking at the insides of his eyelids. He sure didn't look at me. I had a pretty good idea of how Morgan would have summed up the situation: classic passive-aggressive behavior. That's how Morgan summed up a lot of situations.

Finally, in one surprisingly graceful motion, Nick swung his legs over the bench of the picnic table, got up, and turned to face me. He stood so close that I had to tilt my head to meet his eyes. He'd done that to me once before. He was probably in the habit of doing it, to intimidate whomever he was talking to. This time I didn't back up. He jerked his head to the left. I followed him away from the picnic table. When we were out of range of the others, he said, "What do you want?"

When I had decided to talk to him, I'd struggled with what to say. What I'd settled on was: "If you give it back right now, I won't say anything to Kathy."

The skin around his eyes tightened. "Give *what* back?"

"I saw you in the office," I said. Straight-and-narrow people, like my mother, would have called that a lie. More creative people, like my father, would have called it a bluff.

"What office?" Nick said.

He didn't look or sound like he cared one way or the other about me or what I was saying. Maybe he was a better liar than I was. Or a better bluffer.

"The office where all the money is," I said. "I know you took some. If you give it back right now, I won't tell Kathy."

He reacted by not reacting—he just stood there. He didn't say a word. He didn't give any indication that he had even heard me.

"I'm not kidding," I said.

He shook his head in disgust. "Man, and they say people change. You sure haven't."

"Neither have you."

He looked at me—*studied* me—before finally saying, "You didn't see me in that office." He said it as if it were a fact, as if he had no doubts about it. "If you had, you would have gone to Kathy already. You probably would have called the cops too. People like you, if they think they've got something on you, they go straight to the cops. The only time they ever try to make a deal is when they have no proof, when they're trying to make you trip yourself up. But this time you got nothing on me."

This time.

"Yeah? Well, I'm going to talk to Kathy right now," I said.

"You do that," Nick said. He sauntered back to the picnic table and sat down again. The rest of the guys were all over him, probably trying to find out what I had said. Antoine turned and looked at me. I couldn't read his expression any better than I could read Nick's.

I strode back inside, trying to look determined. But Nick was right. I hadn't seen him in the office. I hadn't even seen him in the building. All I had were suspicions—and Nick's track record or, rather, his criminal record. And—this really bothered me—that he hadn't denied it. When an innocent person is accused of stealing, he denies it. At the very least, he becomes indignant. Nick had done neither. Instead, he'd just taunted me.

I hesitated outside my office door and reviewed what facts I had.

Fact: Someone had been in that office and had at least touched that money. There was a good chance that whoever it was had taken some of it.

Fact: The money had been raised for charity. What kind of person would take money that had been raised for a good cause? That was easy—Nick D'Angelo. He'd done it once before.

I walked past my office door and knocked on the one next to it—Kathy's door.

Kathy's expression changed from cheery to expectant to concerned as I spoke. Her shoulders gradually slumped. She caved back in her chair. She asked me a few questions. Finally, she said, "I'll talk to Nick."

"But he's not going to admit it," I said.

Kathy gave me a long, weary look. She seemed disappointed. What shook me was that I wasn't sure who she was disappointed in—Nick, for maybe doing something terrible, or me, for telling her something she clearly did not want to hear. I wished that I hadn't said anything.

CHAPTER **NINE**

"I would have done the same thing," Morgan said when I phoned her at her cottage. "I mean, he's done it before, right? And leopards don't change their spots, right?"

"I guess," I said.

"There's a lesson to be learned here," Morgan said.

There sure was: "Next time I'll lock the door when I leave a room full of money," I said.

She sighed. "Repeat after me, Robyn: I will never, *ever*, participate in one of Billy's crazy animal rights protests again. No good ever comes of them. Animals are still losing the war with people. And it sounds like you're not exactly having the time of your life. *And* I'm bored out of my skull up here without you."

Morgan's endorsement of what I had done should have made me feel better. But it didn't. Morgan tended to be quick to judge others—and her judgments were often harsh. So I sought a second opinion.

"How much did he take?" Billy said, sounding horrified that someone had actually been greedy enough—twice!—to steal money that was intended to help our four-legged friends (and some two-legged ones, if you counted the ducks I had seen on my first day).

"I'm not exactly sure," I said. "That's the point, Billy. I'm not even sure that any money was stolen. But I know that someone was in that office and that someone touched the money." I explained to him exactly what had happened.

There was a long silence on the other end of the phone.

"Billy?"

"I'm still here," he said. More silence. "So you reported this guy, Nick, even though you didn't see him take anything, you didn't even see him in the room or see him come out of the room, and you don't actually know if any money is missing because it hadn't been counted." He sounded doubtful. "But you're pretty sure he stole some of it because it looks like someone touched it and he did something similar back in junior high. Right?"

"Morgan says she would have done the same thing I did."

"Oh," Billy said. Another pause. "Well, maybe she's right."

Maybe.

"What would you have done, Billy? Would you have reported him?"

More agonizing silence.

"I don't know," he said at last. "But you've seen the guy in action. You've talked to him. So if you're sure he did it . . ."

Which, of course, was the problem. But I was sure that *someone* had been in the office and that whoever it was had touched that money. I told myself that Morgan was right—leopards don't change their spots.

.   .   .

After lunch the next day, Janet came into my office and announced that she had an assignment for me. I followed her to a large meeting room where a group of people I didn't know were unpacking boxes of printed materials onto two long tables.

"Welcome to our bimonthly stuff-a-thon," Janet said.

"Stuff-a-thon?"

"We're assembling information kits—tip sheets for pet owners, information about the work we do and, most importantly, a coupon that people can use to send us a donation. We send a kit to anyone who phones or writes asking for information. We also take them with us when we do presentations and displays. Every couple of months we get a group of volunteers together to assemble a few hundred more," she said. When we settled in to work, Janet bustled away. The staff at the shelter always seemed so busy.

It took us a couple of hours to stuff all the information sheets into the animal shelter's colorful folders. I was just tidying up after the rest of the volunteers had left when Kathy appeared. She had a small group of men and women with her. They were all dressed as though they had just stepped out of one of the office towers downtown. Kathy was telling them about some of the shelter's programs. I wondered if they were important donors. Or maybe they were from the government. According to the information kits that I had just finished assembling, the shelter relied on government grants for some of its programs. Kathy was telling the group about how much the shelter relied on volunteers—volunteer dog walkers, volunteer fund-raisers, and volunteer pet-adoption counselors. While she was talking, she glanced out the window. The friendly expression on her face gave way to barely contained fury. She excused herself from her group and came over to me.

"I need you to do something for me, Robyn," she said. "Nick is over there by the fence." She nodded toward the window. "Go and tell him I want to see him in my office *now*, okay? Tell him to wait for me there."

Taken aback by her anger, I hurried outside to fetch Nick. I wondered if Kathy wanted to talk to him about the money. Maybe the volunteers at the mall had had a rough idea of how much they had collected. Maybe Kathy had talked to them and figured out that some of the money was missing.

As soon as I got outside, I saw that Nick wasn't alone. He was talking to someone on the other side of the fence. As I started toward them, he took something out of his backpack and pushed it through the chain-link. Even from where I was standing, I could see what it was. Money. A roll of it.

Nick had passed the roll to a guy with reddish hair who looked vaguely familiar, although I couldn't remember where I had seen him before. He took the money and stuffed it into his jeans pocket.

"Thanks a million, Nick," he said. "It's the last time, I swear. A buddy of mine told me he'd talk to his boss. He's sure the guy will hire me as soon as I get my license back—" He broke off when he spotted me and nodded at Nick, who turned and glared at me.

"What do you want?" he said.

"Kathy said to tell you that she wants to see you in her office," I said. "Right now."

He glanced back at the shelter. He didn't look as calm and cool as he had the day before when I had accused him of stealing. If anything, he looked panicked. *Good*, I thought. He turned back to the guy on the other side of the fence.

"You gotta get out of here," he said.

The guy on the other side of the fence laughed. "Man, they really got you whipped, Nicky," he said.

"*Now*, Joey," Nick said.

Joey.

Nick had talked on the phone last week to someone named Joey. He'd told him to relax, that he'd get it. Did he owe money to this Joey? And the thick roll of cash I had seen him pass through the fence—where would a guy like Nick get that much money? It looked like I hadn't been wrong about him after all. It looked like he really had taken some of the money collected by shelter volunteers.

Joey shrugged, a long, lazy who-cares gesture, before turning and bounding across the open field on the other side of the fence. Nick watched him go. When his eyes met mine again, they were hard and distant. He slipped his other arm through his backpack and brushed past me.

I trailed behind him, not eager to catch up, and hung back when he yanked on the door to go inside. I waited a few moments before going inside myself. As I headed for my office, I heard voices.

"You know better than that," Kathy was saying. She sounded annoyed.

I heard Nick respond: "It's not my fault."

"That doesn't cut it with me, Nick," Kathy said. "And it won't cut it with Ed, either. You're lucky that I spotted Joey before he did. He'd have you out of the program today if he knew." I heard a long sigh followed by a few moments of silence.

"You're not going to tell him, are you?" Nick said. He sounded scared.

"Give me one reason why I shouldn't," Kathy said.

"Joey's not what you think. He's not a bad guy."

"He knows he's not on your approved list, doesn't he? And he knows what happens if you break the rules, right?" Kathy said. "But he's such a good guy that he just ignores all of that, even if it gets *you* in trouble. Is that what you're telling me?"

When Nick spoke again, his voice was small, as if he were a little boy instead of a big, tough teenager.

"Please, Kathy," he said. "Don't tell Mr. Jarvis, okay? Joey just needed some help and I couldn't say no." *Right*, I thought. Joey needed money, and Nick knew exactly where to find some. "It'll never happen again, I promise." He was begging her. I couldn't believe it. Tough guy Nick D'Angelo was actually begging. I wished I could have seen it with my own eyes.

I hoped that Kathy would tell him the same thing I would have if I were in her shoes: Sorry, Nick, but rules are rules. Why should Nick keep getting so many chances to break them?

I heard another long sigh.

"You've mostly been doing well here," Kathy said.

"I have?" There was a note of hope in Nick's voice.

"Although you could have been nicer to Mr. Schuster."

"He doesn't like me." Good-bye hope, hello resentment. "He doesn't even know me. He doesn't know any of us, but he doesn't like us."

"Have you given him any reason to? Any of you?"

Silence.

"You slammed into him, Nick. I know, I know. It was an accident. But he took a bad fall. He's seventy-one years old. And getting you to apologize was like pulling teeth. What would you think if you were in his shoes?"

A few seconds ticked before Nick said, "So, how is he, anyway?"

"He's going to be okay. It wasn't a stroke or a heart attack or anything like that. Just overexertion. He has to rest for a few days, and then he'll be back."

"Are you going to tell Mr. Jarvis about Joey?"

"If you promise me that I won't see Joey around here ever again, I'll let it go this time. But this is your absolute last chance, Nick. I mean it. Okay?"

"Okay."

There was a long silence. Then Kathy said, "You know the money from the fund-raiser that you and Antoine and Trevor carried in yesterday?" I caught my breath. She was going to do it. She was going to confront him. "After I sent you guys back to group, did you go in that office again, Nick? Did you touch the money?"

"No," Nick said, without hesitating even a split second. He didn't sound indignant or wounded or even angry. Mostly he just sounded quiet and, if I hadn't known him better, sincere. I wondered if he'd been prepared for the question.

"Okay, then," Kathy said after a moment. She sounded relieved by his answer, and again, I got the feeling that she didn't want to hear anything negative about him. I wondered why. "You'd better get back before Ed sends out a search party."

I scurried into my office, dropped down in front of my computer, and started pounding away at the keyboard. A moment later, I heard footsteps. They stopped right outside my door. I looked up and saw Nick standing there, watching me. He kept staring at me after my eyes met his. His face was expressionless. He didn't say a word. Then he shook his head and walked away.

CHAPTER **TEN**

I could have taken the subway and the bus to and from the animal shelter. It would have been a lot slower than going by car—the bus didn't travel on the highway—but I wouldn't have minded that much. It wasn't as though I had anything better to do, except sleep in. But my mother insisted on driving me and picking me up on the days that she could swing it, probably because she worked long hours and felt bad that we didn't have a lot of time together. On the days that she couldn't manage it, she'd say, "Call your father. He'll drive you." The next day was one of those days.

"I can take you this morning, but I have a meeting this afternoon," my mother said when I came down for breakfast. "I won't be home until seven. Call your father and ask him to pick you up."

My father asked why my mother wasn't picking me up. I told him. My mother frowned as she listened to me. I was ignoring her prime directive. I was telling my father something about her. My father said okay, he'd be there, no problem.

I was sitting in my broom closet of an office a little later, giving Kathy an update on my progress, when I happened to glance up. By now I knew that the RAD program ran four days a week, Monday, Tuesday, Thursday, and Friday. This was Wednesday, so I was surprised to see a familiar figure stroll past my door. So surprised that I said, "What's he doing here?"

"Who?" Kathy said. She looked over her shoulder at the door, but by then he was gone.

"Nick D'Angelo," I said.

"Oh," Kathy said. "He volunteers here on Wednesdays." Volunteering? Nick? I guess I looked surprised because Kathy said, "Nick was a volunteer here long before he enrolled in the RAD program. He's been volunteering with us for, let's see, almost a year and a half now, I think. Despite everything else that's going on in his life, he's stuck with it. He's been here every Wednesday all summer. He's a good kid."

"But he's—" I stopped myself. I had been going to say that he was in the RAD program because he'd been in serious trouble. But I realized that I didn't actually know what he had done to end up in the program.

"He's what?" Kathy said.

I shook my head and looked back at the files we had been reviewing, but I still felt Kathy's eyes on me. "You shouldn't judge people too quickly, Robyn" she said.

"Especially young people. Just because someone does a couple of stupid things, that doesn't mean his life's course is set and can't be changed."

I wasn't sure what she was referring to. Did she mean whatever Nick had done to end up in the RAD program? Or did she mean something else?

"Nick told me what happened when you two were at school together," Kathy said.

"He did?" I would have thought that was something he'd want to keep to himself.

She nodded. "A couple of days after you started here. I've gotten to know Nick fairly well. I know he's not perfect—who is? But he tries. I think he wanted to be the one to tell me." She looked me in the eye. "He also told me he didn't touch any of the money we collected at the mall," she said. "And I believe him. Okay?"

Everything I'd sensed had been right. Kathy liked Nick. She was willing to give him the benefit of the doubt.

"Okay," I said. Then, mostly to change the subject, I said, "When you first told me about RAD, you said that the kids in the program were each paired with a dog and that it was up to them to train the dogs and to teach them the right kind of behavior so that they'd have a chance of being adopted," I said. "You said if the kids in the RAD program didn't succeed, if the dogs didn't learn how to behave properly, then the dogs might, well . . . You said you might have to put the dogs down." Kathy waited for me to get to the point. "But the first week I was here, I saw Mr. Schuster working with Nick's dog."

Kathy eyed me speculatively and then shook her head. "Mr. Schuster has his own ideas about how things should work," she said. "He's interested in adopting Orion. So if I don't pay close attention, he'll give Orion extra training to hurry along his progress. I've asked him not to, but . . ." She shrugged. "He's promised not to do it again."

.   .   .

At noon, I took my sandwich, my drink, and a book outside, as usual. I was settling in at the picnic table when I saw Nick come out of the Adoption Center with a man, a woman, and a small girl. Nick's hands gestured toward the animal wing, the dog-training area, and the clinic. It looked like he was giving them a tour of the place. Maybe he was going to show them the animals that were up for adoption. I turned my attention back to my book.

I had finished two chapters and was on my way back inside when I heard a shriek. I spun around. The same little girl I had seen earlier was standing on the grass behind me, shaking her head frantically as she clung to her mother's hand. And no wonder. Right in front of the very small girl was a very big dog—Orion. The little girl was obviously unfamiliar with the principles of dog-bite avoidance. She was staring, wide-eyed and terrified, right at Orion. Fortunately, Nick had a firm grip on Orion's leash.

Nick dropped to his knees in front of the girl and slipped an arm around Orion's neck.

"You don't have to be afraid of this guy, Laura," he said.

Laura kept shaking her head. No way was she going to buy that. She may have been young, but she clearly had good instincts.

"I'm going to show you something," Nick said. He stood up. "Watch this."

Curious, I watched too.

"Sit," Nick said. Orion plunked his rear end down on the ground. "Good sit," Nick said. He slipped a treat into the big dog's mouth. "Lie down," Nick said. Orion dropped the front of his body down onto the grass. "Up," Nick said.

The little girl, who had been watching closely when Orion sat and then lay down, pressed herself against her mother when Orion got to his feet again. Nick smiled at her before making Orion sit once more.

"Shake a paw," he said.

Orion extended one of his paws. Nick turned to the little girl and asked her if she wanted to shake it. At first she said no. Her mother shook Orion's paw instead. When nothing bad happened to her, the little girl tried. After Orion had dropped his paw, she pressed up against her mother again. Nick explained to her that dogs are different from people. He said that people recognize other people by what they look like—the shape of their face, the color of their eyes, the size of their nose—but that dogs remember things by smell.

"That's why they're always sniffing each other," he said, "and why they've always got their noses to the ground. They can smell if other dogs have been around. They can even tell which dogs." He extended a hand to Orion's nose. "That's how they remember people too. By smell. You want to meet Orion, Laura?"

Laura looked up at her mother and then over at Nick. She hesitated but finally nodded.

"Give me your hand," Nick said. Again, Laura looked up at her mother, and then over at Nick. He gently took her hand in his. Slowly he brought both hands closer to Orion. Laura looked from Nick to Orion and back again. Nick smiled at her. "He'll smell you and then next time you see him, he'll know you," he said.

Nick guided her hand again, and Laura patted Orion on the head.

"See his tail wagging?" he said. "He likes you."

A smile lit the little girl's face, like sunshine breaking through a cloudy sky. She looked up at her mother, beaming.

"I know you're going to take a kitten home with you," Nick said to her. "And I think that's great. But dogs are pretty cool too. They're loyal. They like to be around people. They're smart. You can teach them all kinds of things. Who knows? Maybe one day you'll decide to get a dog, too." He stood up again. "It's been nice meeting you, Laura. Good luck with your kitten."

Laura reached out, slowly but confidently, and patted Orion again. She and her mother headed back toward the adoption center. Nick smiled and scratched Orion behind one ear, but when he looked over at me, his expression changed. I opened the door and went inside.

· · ·

My father's car was in the parking lot when I finished work. He leaned against it, talking to Mr. Jarvis. He grinned when he saw me. My father is a serious grinner. My mother says he does it to look charming. She says once you get to know him, you realize that charm is more than just an expression on a person's face. Personally, I like his grin. It makes him look like a big, goofy kid.

"How's it going, Robbie?" he said. "Have you met Ed Jarvis?" Before I could answer, he said to Mr. Jarvis, "This is my daughter, Ed. She just narrowly escaped falling into your clutches."

"Oh?" Mr. Jarvis said. He regarded me with new interest. He was probably reevaluating me.

"If her mother hadn't intervened, Robbie could have wound up with a record," my father said.

Oh, great. He was going to tell Mr. Jarvis the so-called ironic story of how I had ended up volunteering at the animal shelter.

"Dad," I said, hoping to hurry him along to the car before he could get started.

"If an ex-police officer and a lawyer can't raise a law-abiding citizen, what hope is there?" my father said, oblivious to my tugs on his arm.

"Dad, we should go."

But it was too late. My father launched into his story. I turned around to head for the car and found myself face-to-face with Nick. Like Mr. Jarvis, he was looking at me with new interest. His eyes moved from me to my father's ebony Porsche and back to me.

"Nick," Mr. Jarvis said. "My car is over there. I'll be with you in a minute." He tossed Nick a set of keys.

Nick caught the keys easily, even though his eyes were fixed on me. What was that expression on his face? A smirk? A sneer? I circled my father's car, yanked open the passenger-side door, got inside, and slammed the door as hard as I could. That got my father's attention. He hates it when people slam the doors of his precious car. He shot me a look—no charm visible now—said good-bye to Mr. Jarvis.

"Someone's in a bad mood," he said.

"*Someone* doesn't appreciate her father discussing her personal life with a complete stranger," I said.

"Ed isn't a stranger. I've known him for years. He works with probation cases."

I gave him a look that I had learned from my mother— narrowed eyes, taut mouth, head tilted slightly to one side. It was a look that said, Who do you think you're kidding?

"He's a stranger to *me*," I said.

"Okay," my father said. "I'm sorry. Tell you what? How about if I make it up to you by taking you out for dinner?"

I glanced at the bouquet of flowers on the back seat, their stems carefully wrapped in a layer of damp newspaper surrounded by a protective sheet of plastic.

"It looks like you have other plans," I said.

"The only plan I have," he said, "is to spend some quality time with my daughter."

Hmmm. August. Flowers in the back seat. A declared interest in quality time with me. And the fact that my mother wouldn't be pulling into her driveway until around seven—about the same time my father would be dropping me off if he took me out to dinner first.

"Forget it, Dad," I said.

He turned the key in the ignition. "Forget what?" His face was pure innocence—if you overlooked the mischievous twinkle in his eyes.

"Forget that it's the anniversary of when you met Mom or the anniversary of your first actual date with her or whatever." I could never remember exactly which it was. "If you show up at the house with flowers, she's only going to get angry."

Most people would take divorce as the final rejection. Not my father. He still acted as if my mother were playing hard to get. He gazed out the Porsche's tinted windshield as if he were peering into a happier past.

"That first night we had dinner together, I knew she was the one for me," he said. "She still is."

"She divorced you, Dad."

"Temporary setback," he said.

See what I mean?

"Four years of not living together doesn't sound temporary to me, Dad."

"You're young," he said as he backed up the Porsche. "Four years is nothing. Things have been going really well for me, Robbie. Your mother was right. Quitting the police force was a smart thing to do."

Too bad he had done it only after my mother had kicked him out of the house. I think that had made her even angrier. When my father was a police officer, he was never home. When my mother went back to school to get her law degree, she complained that she might as well be a single parent. She wanted him to be there for her the way she had been there for him. They fought all the time.

"She asked me if you could stay with me this weekend instead of next weekend," he said, oh-so-casually. "You have any idea why?"

"I think she's going on a business trip," I said. Actually, I knew she was. I also knew it was a business trip of Ted's, but I didn't tell him that.

He glanced at me and smiled, but he didn't fool me. He was wondering if he could push a little more. He decided to give it a shot.

"What kind of business trip?"

"Lawyer stuff, I guess," I said. "To be honest, Dad," which, to be honest, I wasn't being, "I sort of tune out when she starts talking about work."

I looked directly at him when I said that. Ex-cops are the same as cops—they think they can read you by reading your eyes. And maybe they can, if they're not your father and they don't blatantly dote on you and they can't imagine that you would ever be less than truthful with them. My father stopped quizzing me, we went out for dinner, and then he drove me home. Of course he pulled right into the driveway and followed me up to the front door. Of course he didn't stay on the porch like he should have, given that he wasn't supposed to enter unless my mother invited him. And of course, when he heard dishes rattling in the kitchen, he pushed past me and strode in, bouquet first.

"Is that you, Robyn?" my mother said, except that her voice didn't come from the kitchen. It came from the door to her study. I took a deep breath and told her the last thing she wanted to hear.

"Dad's here."

I couldn't have made her smile disappear any faster if it had been chalk and my words were an eraser. She glanced around, trying to figure out exactly where he was. I nodded toward the kitchen. She marched down the hall and through the kitchen door. I followed her.

My father was standing face-to-face with Ted Gold. Well, actually, it was more like face to chest—Ted's face to my father's chest. My father is taller than average. Ted is more on the height-challenged side. My father was giving him the famous Mac Hunter once-over. What started as a look of disapproving surprise changed to one of frank amusement as he inventoried Ted's attributes: short, slightly paunchy (Ted loves to cook—and eat), thinning hair, apron around his waist, shirtsleeves pushed up, pot scrubber in his hand. Ted was the diametric opposite of my father.

"Mac," my mother said sternly.

My father tore his eyes away from Ted. When he swung around to face my mother, he was grinning confidently.

"Patti," he said, his voice full of affection. "How are you?"

"Patricia," My mother corrected—again.

"These are for you," my father said, thrusting the bouquet of flowers at her.

My mother's hands remained at her sides. Her face was decidedly lacking in affection. "You're not supposed to be here, Mac," she said.

If my father caught the chill in her voice, he gave no sign of it. If anything, his grin broadened. He reached up into the cupboard above the fridge and grabbed a vase, which he carried to the sink and filled with water. Ted, of course, stepped aside for him, which earned him a blast of my mother's frigid expression. That was my father for you. My mother used to say that when he was young, he was one of those kids who got everyone else in trouble while he sailed through the world on a sea of innocent charm.

My father plunked the flowers into the vase and set it on the table.

"Memories, Patti," he said. "What would we be without them?"

"Happy," my mother said.

My father had the ability to overlook or ignore anything that didn't fit into his plans. He acted as if he hadn't heard her.

"I was just getting acquainted with Ted," he said.

"Good-bye, Mac," my mother said.

"Did Patti ever tell you how we met?" my father said to Ted.

"*Good-bye*, Mac," my mother said again. She moved toward the kitchen door, signaling him that he should do likewise.

My father glanced at me. I shrugged.

"Well," my father said. He was still smiling. "I guess I'd better run along."

My mother waited in stony silence for him to do just that. My father dropped a kiss onto the top of my head before he left the room. My mother stared at me. Together we heard the front door open and close again, then a car door open and close, and an engine turn over. I know exactly what my mother was thinking: *How could you, Robyn?* As if I had any more control over my father than she did.

"So that's the infamous Mackenzie Hunter," Ted said. "He seems like a charming fellow." He sounded sincere. I figured this was a good time to make myself scarce.

. . .

My father's unexpected visit put my mother in a bad mood. Two days later she was still railing against him. Who did he think he was, she said as she drove me to the shelter, barging into her house like that (even though he hadn't actually barged—it had been more like a saunter)? Who did he think he was, interrogating her like that (even though he hadn't really interrogated—the only thing he had asked was how she was, and he had done that while offering her a bouquet of flowers)? Who did he think he was, intimidating Ted like that (even though Ted had seemed more charmed than intimidated)?

"Relax, Mom," I said. "You're going away this afternoon, remember?" She was looking forward to her weekend with Ted. "Have you packed?"

She nodded. "You are *not* to tell your father about this, Robyn. Understand?"

"But he's already met Ted," I said. In fact, if I knew my father, he'd probably done a thorough background check on Ted. He probably knew more about Ted than Ted's own mother did.

"Robyn." She drew out the two syllables of my name so that it was a plea and a warning all in one. I raised my left hand and laid my right hand over my heart.

"I swear I won't say a thing, Mom."

Later, while I checked and entered names, I thought about the weekend. Billy had already told me he was busy—the activist camp counselors were all going to an activist conference. Morgan was still up in cottage country. Which left...well, I wasn't sure what it left. Probably another dull weekend. I was feeling sorry for myself when Kathy appeared with a thick envelope.

"Can you do me a favor, Robyn?" she said. "I'm just going into a meeting and Janet's off today. Ed—Mr. Jarvis—was supposed to have signed these grant applications, but I guess he forgot. He should be out behind the animal wing, getting ready for the group. Can you find him and get his signature? Then seal the envelope and call a courier. If these applications aren't sent out right away, we're going to miss the deadline. Okay?"

"No problem," I said.

Mr. Jarvis was exactly where Kathy had said he would be. He pulled the sheaf of papers out the envelope, signed all the documents where Kathy had indicated with yellow sticky notes, shoved everything back into the envelope and handed it to me. I started back to the office. As I was rounding the side of the building, I heard a yelp. I turned the corner to see Antoine holding a leash and kicking the dog at the other end of it. The dog yelped again and strained on the leash, trying to get away from Antoine.

"Hey!" I said. "Stop that!"

The dog, which had been cringing, sprang to attention when it saw me. It continued to pull on its leash, except that now it was pulling toward me, snarling. Antoine seemed to enjoy that.

"Looks like the dog and me agree on one thing," he said. "We agree that you should get lost."

"You're supposed to be training that dog so that it can get adopted," I said, seething. "You're *not* supposed to be kicking it, as I'm sure Kathy and Mr. Jarvis would agree."

While I was talking, Antoine was gathering in the dog's leash until, finally, he had the dog by its collar.

"You threatening me?" he said. "You gonna get me into trouble?"

The dog that I had taken pity on was growling now and pulling even harder to get free of Antoine. The only thing that kept it from hurtling at me was Antoine's hand, and Antoine was slowly but surely loosening his grip. I watched as one finger came away from the collar and then another. My legs started to shake. I tried to hide what I was feeling, but I must not have been doing a very good job because Antoine smiled.

"You know how the RAD dogs ended up here, right?" he said. "Same way the RAD guys did. They hurt people. And you know what they told us when we started with this program? That not all these dogs were gonna make it. They said they were giving the dogs a second chance but that sometimes a second chance isn't enough." He removed another finger from the dog's collar so that now there was only one finger and one thumb restraining the animal. "This dog here, maybe he's not going to make it. Maybe this is his big chance, right now, to prove himself. And maybe he's going to fail."

His index finger slid away from the dog's collar. The dog-bite rules kicked in and I backed up slowly, careful not to meet the dog's eyes, careful not to challenge it.

"Knock it off, Antoine," a voice behind me said. "And get a grip on that dog. *Now.*"

Someone—Nick—strode past me, grabbed the dog's leash, and thrust it into Antoine's hand.

"Are you crazy?" he said to Antoine. "You know what she's going to do?" He nodded stiffly in my direction. "She's going to run inside and tell on you. Is that what you want? You want to screw this up?" He sounded disgusted. He grabbed Antoine's shoulder and shoved him. "Get out of here," he said. "Get to group."

Antoine scowled at me, but he tightened his hand on the leash and led the dog toward the animal wing. Nick waited until he was almost there before turning to me.

"Everything's okay now, right?" he said. "You weren't hurt, so there's no problem, right?" There was an angry bite to his voice.

"Everything's *not* okay," I said. "He was hurting that dog. He kicked it. Twice."

Nick shook his head. Was that disappointment I saw on his face?

"Look," he said, "I'll keep an eye on him, okay? I'll make sure he doesn't do it again. So you don't have to say anything, okay?"

Not okay, I thought. I started back toward my office. When I got there, I was going to report Antoine. He didn't deserve to be in the RAD program.

Nick grabbed my arm.

"Hey!" I said. I spun around to face him.

He let go of me.

"Give him one more chance," he said. "That's all I'm asking. Just one more chance."

"Why should I?" I said. "The RAD program is supposed to help dogs behave better so that they can be adopted. Abusing a dog isn't going to make it more people-friendly. In fact, I don't think somebody who abuses animals should be allowed to stay in the program. So if you think I'm going to close my eyes and pretend I didn't see what I saw, you're wrong."

"That figures," he muttered.

Jerk, I thought. I started back to the office again. He stepped in front of me, blocking my way.

"Wait," he said.

"What for?"

"I know what you think," he said.

I seriously doubted that.

"You think we're a bunch of losers," he said. "I bet you're not even all that surprised that Antoine kicked his dog. You probably think we all do the same thing the minute Ed's back is turned."

Okay, so maybe he did have a pretty good idea what I thought. Well, mostly. I had seen him with Orion enough times to know—well, maybe to believe—that he would never hurt a dog.

We stood there, staring at each other, not trusting each other, Nick's glare making it clear that he didn't like me. Then he stepped back and looked down at the ground for a moment.

"Okay," he said finally. "Maybe Antoine's been having some problems." His tone was marginally softer.

"Maybe?"

"If you knew him, you'd know he was making progress."

"Kicking a dog is progress?"

He looked at me the way you'd look at a tourist. Like I was someone with a tenuous grasp of the local language and customs.

"He gets frustrated," he said. "He's used to working out his frustrations physically. That's why he's here."

"Oh," I said. "So what you're saying is, it's okay if he kicks a dog because it's not his fault. It's what he's used to. Is that it?"

He shook his head. "No, that's not it," he said, his voice patient now, as if he had decided it was worth the effort to attempt to explain to this tourist how things worked. "I'm just trying to tell you about Antoine. Because if he gets kicked out of this program, it's not going to be good for him."

It might be good for his dog, I thought. But I didn't say that. Instead, I said, "Fine," and crossed my arms over my chest. "So tell me."

He looked at me for a moment, frowning a little, as if he was trying to figure out where to start.

"Antoine lives with his mother and his kid brother, who's seven," he said finally. "And with whatever boyfriend his mom happens to bring home. The latest *boyfriend*"—he made the word sound like an insult—"when he gets mad, he likes to take it out on other people. Mostly smaller people. I bet you don't know any guys like that, do you?"

I didn't, but I didn't tell Nick that. I didn't say anything.

"Besides being a bully, the guy's an idiot. Took a swing at a cop who pulled him over for speeding. When Antoine got his sentence, the boyfriend was in lockup. Antoine's in open custody now, in a group home. The boyfriend, though, he just got out. He's back at Antoine's house, with Antoine's mother and Antoine's brother. Antoine only found out this morning when his kid brother called him, crying."

Oh.

"That still doesn't make it okay for Antoine to kick his dog," I said. "Or to threaten me."

"No kidding," Nick said. His face was grim. He glanced around, checking to see if anyone could hear us. "But he's not what you think," he said. "He's not a bad guy. He deserves another chance."

He sounded just like Kathy when she had described the RAD dogs.

"And you want *me* to give him that chance?" I said.

"I know it's not your style. But would it kill you?"

I stared at him. Okay, so maybe he wasn't as bad as Antoine. Maybe he wouldn't take his frustration out on a dog. And maybe Kathy liked him and believed him when he said he hadn't taken any money. But he was still the person I had caught back in junior high running out of the office with charity money. He'd just taken it. Taken it and spent it. He was here at the animal shelter now because he had been charged and convicted of some kind of violent crime. And what about the roll of bills that I had seen him slip through the fence to his friend Joey? Kathy saw one side of him—the side that he chose to show her. I saw another side. For all I knew, he could be making up a sob story about his friend just so I wouldn't report him.

"If Antoine's not really a bad guy, what's he doing here?" I said.

"He *volunteered* to be here, same as me," he said, looking hard at me. "Same as you." I felt heat in my cheeks. So he *had* heard what my father had told Mr. Jarvis. "Even good girls can slip up, huh?"

"That's different," I said.

"Yeah. I bet it is."

Boy, even when he wanted something from me, he couldn't help sneering at me.

"I mean, what was Antoine charged with?" I said, trying to stay calm. "What did he do?"

"What difference does it make?"

"You want me to give him a break. So I think I have the right to know."

"I can't tell you."

Right. I started to move around him. He stepped in front of me again.

"Okay," he said. "He warned the guy—the boyfriend—to leave his brother alone."

"*Warned* him?"

"Okay, so maybe he kind of threatened him," Nick said. I waited. Nick watched me for a moment. "Maybe with a knife."

"*Maybe?*"

"He was looking out for his kid brother," Nick said. "Things got a little out of hand. The boyfriend got nicked."

"Got nicked? Like, oops, the knife jumped out of Antoine's hand?"

"*Antoine* nicked him," Nick said, sounding exasperated. "The guy took five stitches."

"And Antoine got charged?"

"Yeah, he got charged. The boyfriend made sure of that. The day before they sent Antoine to the group home, the boyfriend messed up and got arrested. He didn't make bail. He got sentenced to eight months, so Antoine relaxed a little. He knew the guy wasn't going to mess with his brother. But now the guy's out and he's back living with Antoine's mother."

"And that's why Antoine kicked his dog? He was taking out his anger on him?"

"Yeah," Nick said. "And yeah, I know he has to stop acting the way he does. But if you ask me, the boyfriend has to stop taking things out on little kids. And Antoine's mother has to maybe think about the guys she's spending time with." He shook his head in frustration. "Look, I promise he'll never hurt the dog again. If he does, *I'll* report him. Hell, you can report *me* too if you want. I don't care. All I'm asking is that you give him one more chance."

Give one more chance to a guy who had attacked another guy with a knife? This really was foreign territory. And it sure made me wonder.

"What about you?" I said.

"What about me?"

"What are you doing here?"

Nick's eyes turned to ice, and there was a chill in his voice when he answered.

"We're not talking about me," he said. "We're talking about Antoine. Are you going to tell on him or what?"

I met his cold eyes and told him exactly what I was thinking. "I don't know," I said.

He shook his head in disgust. "Yeah, well, whatever, princess," he said. "I'm not going to get down on my knees and beg."

As if I had asked him to.

He started to turn away.

"Hey, Nick?"

He looked over his shoulder at me.

"Where did you get the money you gave your friend Joey?"

For a second he almost looked hurt. Then he wheeled around and stalked away.

CHAPTER **ELEVEN**

Kathy was still in her meeting when I got back to my desk. I couldn't have told her what Antoine had done even if I'd wanted to, and I wasn't sure I wanted to. What if Nick had been telling the truth? What if Antoine had the kind of home life that I couldn't even imagine? What would happen if I told? Would he get kicked out of the program? Then what would happen to him?

Did I even care?

I guess I did, because when Kathy dropped by my office after her meeting, I told her that Mr. Jarvis had signed the grant applications and that the courier had already picked them up, guaranteeing delivery of her grant proposal by the end of the day. And that was all I told her.

Later, when I went to the staff kitchen to wash out my mug, I heard Nick's voice inside. While I waited out in the hall for him to leave, I heard him say, "He's been doing really good."

"Really *well*," Kathy corrected in a gentle voice. "I know. Both Ed and Stella have told me."

Who were they talking about? Was Nick telling her about Antoine? Was he afraid that I would say something?

"So," Nick said, drawing out the word, sounding like a nervous little kid, "I was wondering, you know, about after."

"After?"

"After the program is over. I was wondering . . . if Orion keeps on the way he has been, you know, if he succeeds in the program . . ."

He wasn't talking about Antoine after all. He was talking about the big dog.

Kathy laughed. "You're leading somewhere, Nick, I can feel it. Spit it out."

Silence, followed by a rush of words. "It's about finding a good home for Orion," Nick said. "I want to know if *I* can adopt him, you know, if he keeps doing as great as he has been doing."

More silence. I wished I could see the look on Kathy's face. Was she surprised by Nick's question, or had she been expecting it?

Finally, she said, "Orion isn't the only one who has been doing well. Ed says you take the program seriously. So does Stella. She told me that you've been studying up on dogs. She said that with all the reading you've been doing, you know almost as much as she does."

I remembered Nick sitting at the picnic table with his book and highlighting pen. I wondered if he paid as much attention in school as he did to that book.

"And Ed says that the rest of the boys look up to you," Kathy said. "He says you've been a good influence."

Silence from Nick. Then a sound like a sigh.

"But, Nick, you know the policy. Your job—the job of all RAD participants—is to train the dogs so that they're ready for other people to adopt, not so that you can adopt them yourselves. Besides, they don't allow pets at the group home."

Nick lived in a *group home?* That was news to me. But I really shouldn't have been surprised. After all, he was here because he had been in trouble with the law.

"I know," Nick said. "But what if I knew someone who was interested in adopting him? What would they have to do to make it happen?"

"I don't understand," Kathy said.

Neither did I.

"I told my aunt all about Orion. She wants to meet him. She's coming here this afternoon to pick me up. She said she might be interested in adopting a dog."

I wondered if the shelter had a policy on relatives of RAD participants adopting dogs that were in the program.

When Kathy spoke again, she sounded surprised. "Your aunt is picking you up? You're not going in the van with the rest of the kids?"

"I'm getting sprung for the weekend," Nick said, his voice buoyant now. "Actually, that's the other thing I was wondering about."

"More wondering," Kathy said with a laugh.

"I got permission to spend the weekend with my aunt. Sort of time off for good behavior," he said. "I was wondering about a little time off for Orion too. I was thinking maybe my aunt and I could take him home for the weekend so she could get acquainted with him. What do you think? She already said it was okay with her if it's okay with you. And she's got a nice place, her own house. It's about a block from a park where they have an off-leash area for dogs." He told Kathy where his aunt lived. I knew the neighborhood. It was in the east end of the city.

"Nick, believe me, if I could say yes, I would. But I can't. You know that. As long as an animal is in our care, it has to stay at the shelter."

"But my aunt has already said she might be willing to adopt him."

"First," Kathy said, "Orion has to succeed in the program—which isn't over yet."

"He *will* succeed," Nick said. "I know he will. He's a good dog."

I pictured Orion—massive, powerful, and fierce. But good? Then I pictured him sitting at Nick's command and extending a paw for a little girl to shake.

"Still," Kathy said, "it wouldn't be fair to expose him to a whole new environment before he's ready. And it wouldn't be fair to your aunt, either. What if Orion forgot himself? What if he reverted to his old behavior?"

"He wouldn't do that," Nick said.

"But if he did, it would leave the shelter open to a lot of problems. It could even jeopardize the RAD program, and I don't think you want that to happen, do you, Nick?"

Silence.

"I'm sorry, Nick, but I'm going to have to say no. And to be honest, I'm not even sure about your aunt adopting him. I'm not sure that fits with the policy."

"You said the policy is that kids in the program can't adopt the dogs. My aunt isn't in the program. I don't even live with her."

"But you're going to," Kathy said. "Isn't that the plan? After you get out of the group home, you're going to live with your aunt."

No answer. Then, "She's coming to pick me up," he said. "I told her I'd introduce her to Orion."

"I think that would be okay," Kathy said. "I'm sure she'd be proud to see how much work you've done with him. Now if you'll excuse me, Nick, I have to get back to work."

I retreated quickly before either of them could see me.

. . .

At the end of the day, as I started across the lawn toward the parking lot, I saw my father with Nick and a woman

I didn't recognize. I guessed she was Nick's aunt. My father was bent over slightly, shaking Orion's paw. Then he spotted me.

"Hey, Robbie," he called. "Come here. You've got to see this."

But by the time I reached them, my father was deep into a story that I wished he'd stop telling.

"*Dad*," I said. If he'd paid the slightest attention, he would have read the warning in my voice. But my father never pays attention when he's regaling an audience. He would have made a great actor, according to my mother. "He certainly has the ego for it," she'd said.

"Small, puppyish teeth," he was saying, "not at all like the teeth on this fine animal here." He patted Orion on the head and didn't even pause, let alone jump (like I did) when Orion sprang to his feet and barked.

"Sit," Nick said firmly.

Orion sat.

"Nipped Robbie's little bottom," my father went on. "The man who owned the dog said that the animal was just being playful—puppies are like babies, they sometimes do the wrong thing, but they're not being malicious—"

"*Dad*," I said again. Even to my ears, I sounded a lot like my mother. Maybe that's why my father did what he always did when *she* tried to caution him. He kept right on talking.

"Anyway, Robbie screamed. She was just a child," he said. "And this puppy, the poor thing got scared and it held on for dear life. Left a little scar back there, if I'm not mistaken." Nick and the woman with him gave me a sympathetic look.

"It was *not* a puppy!" I said. Nothing that big could possibly have been a puppy. "And you weren't even there."

"It must have been traumatic," the woman said.

"Still," my father said, "no harm done, other than a deep-seated fear of dogs. Which is why it's both ironic and, well, maybe even therapeutic that Robbie's little scrape with the law resulted in—"

"*Dad*," I said. I grabbed him by the arm. "We should go."

"In a minute," he said. He turned to the woman. "This is my daughter, Robyn," he said. "Robbie, I guess you've already met Nick. This is his aunt, Beverly Thrasher."

"Call me Bev," Nick's aunt said to my father. He'd charmed another one.

Nick nodded curtly at me.

"Robbie may be the only animal rights advocate in the world who's afraid of the animals she's defending," my father said with a chuckle. "But I give her a lot of credit. She stands up for what she believes in. A few weeks ago, she and her friends were at a protest march . . ."

I sighed. Here we go again. I could try to stop him. While I was at it, I could also stop the sun from setting and Earth from rotating on its axis. I went to lean against his car instead.

At first, Nick stayed to listen to my father's story. But after a few minutes, he led Orion over to where I was standing. I took a step back and avoided meeting the dog's eyes. Now what, I wondered.

"You didn't rat on Antoine," he said.

I didn't say anything.

Nick glanced back at my father. "Your dad seems okay," he said. "You know, for a rich guy. He's pretty funny too."

"He's not all that funny," I said. "Sometimes he's a real pain."

"He likes to tell stories about you, huh?"

What an understatement. "It's like a hobby to him."

"Well, now I get why you're always so nervous."

"Nervous?"

"Around *him*." He nodded to Orion. "Like that first day you were here." He reached down and scratched the animal affectionately behind the ear. The big dog pressed up against Nick's leg, his whole body quivering with pleasure. Nick laughed. "He looks like a dog, but believe me, half the time he acts like a pussy cat."

He grinned at me, and his whole face changed. Most of the time when I saw him, he was deadly serious, like he was thinking about something unpleasant or remembering something bad. And when he was serious, he looked almost dangerous, partly because of the scar that cut like a ribbon across his right cheek. I wondered how long he had had it and how he had got it. But when he smiled, the scar seemed to vanish. Instead of looking like a guy who was ready to pound on someone out in the school yard, he looked like a kid who had just earned a gold star from the teacher.

"He's doing great in the program," he said with pride.

"That's nice," I said. I knew that Mr. Schuster saw something promising in the big dog. And Nick sure seemed taken with him. But you couldn't have paid me enough to adopt a beast like that.

A hand fell on my shoulder. My father's hand.

"Come on, Robbie. You'd better get a move on, or we'll get stuck in rush-hour traffic," he said, as if the delay were my fault.

"We'd better get going too," Nick's aunt said. "Glen will be waiting."

"Glen?" Nick said.

"I told you about Glen," Nick's aunt said. "He's coming over tonight. I thought it was time the two of you finally met."

Nick's face clouded. I wondered who Glen was.

"Well, nice meeting you, Nick," my father said, thrusting out a hand. Nick seemed a little stunned by the gesture, but he shook my father's hand.

.　.　.

When we got back to the loft, my father started to prepare supper. He has a huge kitchen, with a massive gas stove, a stainless steel state-of-the-art refrigerator, every kitchen gadget on the market, and racks of pots and pans. The kitchen, like the rest of the place, had been planned and stocked by the interior designer my father hired when he took over the building. I guess the designer was under the impression that my father's kitchen skills extended beyond making coffee and pouring milk over dry cereal, which at the time they didn't. But in the four years that he'd been living on his own, he had actually learned to cook. I perched on a stool at the counter, watching him throw together black bean quesadillas, which he served with his own special green chili.

"So," he said, not trusting himself to look at me, "I guess your poor mother is holed up all alone in a hotel somewhere by now."

"Very subtle, Dad."

He flashed me the smile that he claimed had won my mother's heart all those years ago. "You think so?"

"No. And I'm not going to talk about her. She hates it when I talk about her."

"Really?" he said, as if this was news to him, which it most certainly was not. "Why? Does she have something to hide?"

"Yes," I said.

My father looked at me again, one eyebrow raised a few millimeters higher than the other.

"She's hiding her private life," I said. "From you. She doesn't think her personal affairs are anyone else's business. And, Dad? I feel the same way."

My father grinned again. "But it's a funny story, Robbie."

"I don't like you telling complete strangers stories about me. Especially when they involve my butt."

He raised his right hand, like a witness swearing an oath. "You have my word, Robbie," he said. "I'll cut my tongue out of my head before I ever tell that story again."

It would have been touching if he hadn't already made that promise—about a hundred times. He dropped some chopped onions into a hot skillet.

"So what's the story with that boy?" he said.

"What boy?"

"The one at the shelter. The kid with the big dog."

"What do you mean, what's the story?"

"He seems like a nice kid. He sure knows dogs."

"Yeah, I guess."

"How did he get that scar?"

"How would I know?"

"You were talking to him. It looked like it wasn't the first time. I thought maybe you two worked together."

"We don't," I said. "I've seen him around, but I don't know him, if you know what I mean."

"Ah," my father said, nodding.

"Ah?' What does that mean?"

"Not a thing."

"Dad—"

"It doesn't mean anything, Robbie. I just saw the way he was looking at you and the way you were looking back, and I wondered if maybe you and he were, you know..."

"*What?*" My father prided himself on his powers of observation. It sounded to me like he needed glasses, because he was definitely misreading the situation. "You thought *I* was interested in *Nick D'Angelo?*"

My father looked surprised by my reaction.

"I guess not, huh?" he said.

"No!"

"Is it because he has that big dog?"

"It's not his dog. It's a shelter dog. And I don't want to talk about it, Dad."

He studied me for a moment.

"Okay," he said.

"Okay."

He went back to cooking. I went back to watching. But I couldn't help it. I had to ask.

"What do you mean, you saw the way he was looking at me?"

My father added some strips of red pepper to the skillet.

"I thought you didn't want to talk about it," he said.

I glared at him.

"Okay," my father said. "I got the impression he was interested in you."

"Interested?"

"You know, like he might want to get to know you better."

"You think *Nick D'Angelo* looked interested in me?"

"Is that so improbable?"

It was. After everything that had happened, I was the last person that Nick would ever be interested in. And vice versa.

"You should get your eyes checked, Dad," I said.

He shrugged and turned back to the stove.

We were halfway through our meal when my father's buzzer sounded. He got up and pressed the intercom button next to the door.

"It's me," a voice said. I recognized it immediately. It was Vern Deloitte, my father's partner in the security business. Like my father, Vern is a former police officer. He's more serious than my father. He's also older. He always complains that now that my father is making money on this old building, he should install an elevator. My father just laughs.

My father pressed another button. This one opened the security door on the main floor. A few moments later, we heard slow, heavy footsteps climbing the concrete factory-like stairs to my father's place.

Vern was breathing hard by the time my father opened the door to let him in. But he smiled broadly when he saw me.

"Hi, Robyn," he said.

"Hi, Vern. Have you had supper yet?"

He had. But he sniffed the air and said, "That sure smells good, though." So I got him a plate and some cutlery and served him some quesadillas.

"What's up, Vern?" my father said. He had finished eating and shoved his plate aside.

Vern glanced at me before turning to my father. "Robyn here for the weekend?" he said.

My father studied Vern. So did I. Vern kept his eyes on his food. I had a pretty good idea what that meant.

"Patti's out of town," my father said.

Vern shoveled some quesadillas into his mouth and chewed and swallowed before he said, "I just got a call from that guy I told you about."

He didn't say what guy. He didn't have to. My father knew. He leaned across the table toward Vern.

"Did he have anything useful?"

Vern nodded as he raised his fork to his mouth again. "Could be something's going to happen pretty soon."

My father nodded. "What's Henri up to this weekend?"

Henri is Henrietta Saint-Onge, Vern's girlfriend. She's a painter. She lives in a 150-year-old house that stands on a piece of land that, according to Vern, is worth millions of dollars. It's located smack in the middle of the financial district. Its neighbors on either side are massive office towers. Even with skylights, Henri has to turn on the lights at noon. Henri subs as a sort of babysitter—a term that at the age of fifteen, I don't appreciate—if my father gets called away when it's his turn to take me for the weekend. The thing my father likes most about Henri is that she's discreet. She never lets on to my mother that she has ever taken responsibility for me. My mother would be furious if she knew. My mother's view is that she's spent a lifetime scheduling her life around my needs and that if my father is at all serious about fatherhood, he should be able to do the same every other weekend or so—never mind that I was perfectly capable of looking after myself.

"She's around," Vernon said. He was careful not to look at me. Vern isn't just my father's partner. He's also his best friend. I couldn't think of anything Vern wouldn't do for my father, except maybe run interference with my mother. I can't prove it, but I think Vern is afraid of her.

I sighed. "Do you want me to go and pack?" I said. I wasn't angry. What was the point? It wouldn't have done any good. Besides, spending the weekend with Henri pretty much guaranteed that I wouldn't be bored. Henri is always working on something interesting, and she always takes the time to try to explain it to me because I usually don't understand. Henri's art is really abstract. When she isn't working, she likes to hang out at cafés. She especially likes cafés that hold poetry readings. It's taken me almost three years, but I'm beginning to see why. Spending the weekend with Henri definitely wouldn't be the end of the world.

My father glanced at Vern, who shrugged. I got up and repacked everything I had unpacked before dinner.

"I'm sorry, Robbie," my father said. "It's probably just for tonight." Vern coughed. "Well, maybe tomorrow too. But I'll be back on Sunday." A glance at Vern told me that he likely wouldn't be.

"Mom said she'd pick me up here Sunday night," I said.

"You have your keys?" he said. I produced them from my pocket. "Good," my father said. "You know, just in case."

Just in case he was tied up with work all weekend. Just in case Henri had to drop me off at my father's place before my mother showed up. My mother never came upstairs to get me. She always called on her cell phone from her car to tell me she was waiting. She would never know that my father wasn't there.

.   .   .

I spent the rest of Friday night with Henri. On Saturday we took the streetcar to the market. It's a dozen blocks of narrow streets and small, colorful shops that sell every type of food you can think of—Chinese vegetables, Indian spices, cheeses of the world, breads and rolls and sweet buns, fish, meat, nuts, fruit. We stocked up on good things to eat before hitting our favorite street, which was no wider than an alley and lined on both sides with old houses whose ground floors had been converted into shops that sell vintage clothing—fifties bowling shirts, sixties miniskirts, and seventies bell-bottoms. Henri assembled her wardrobe exclusively from these stores and from charity thrift shops. She bought a pair of vintage jeans and some cat's eye sunglasses. I tried on dozens of cocktail dresses, but the only thing I bought was a ring.

On Saturday night we went to the Cinématheque to see some Egyptian movies. I had never seen a movie made in Egypt before. That's the neat thing about Henri. She's always getting me to do things I've never done before. On Sunday morning we slept in. Morgan called me on my cell phone right after we'd finished brunch: granola pancakes served with homemade maple-syrup yogurt—recipes that Henri had invented.

"I'm going crazy up here," she said. "I'm starting to feel like Tom Hanks in that movie. You know, the one where he gets stuck on a desert island and has no one to talk to except a basketball?"

"It was a volleyball, Morgan."

"Whatever," Morgan said. "It's dead up here."

Morgan's family's cottage was on an island in the middle of a lake in a) the middle of the most beautiful and peaceful part of cottage country or b) the middle of nowhere—depending on whether Morgan was trying to convince me to go to the cottage with her or whether she was feeling sorry for herself for being there all by her lonesome, which is to say, with no one to talk to except her parents.

"I wish I were back home with you," she said.

"You say that now," I said. "But tomorrow morning while you're sleeping in, I'll be dragging myself up to the animal shelter. And while you're sunning yourself on the dock or cooling off in the lake, I'll be sitting in front of a computer developing a repetitive stress injury from typing in the names and addresses of complete strangers. Then tomorrow evening while you're sitting on the veranda watching the sun set, I'll be thinking about the fact that I have to get up early again the next morning and go back to the animal shelter and sit in front of that computer for another whole day."

"You're the best friend ever," Morgan said, sounding much brighter now. "You always make me feel better."

"Glad to be of service," I said. Just before I hung up, I heard a loon call on the other end of the line. I pictured Morgan against a backdrop of green pine and blue water. Poor thing—all alone in paradise.

.   .   .

Henri drove me to my father's place a little after seven. At exactly eight o'clock my phone rang. It was my mother. I grabbed my overnight bag and ran down to meet her.

"How was your weekend?" she asked.

I shrugged. "You know Dad. How was yours?"

Her smile was radiant, but all she said was "Fine."

CHAPTER **TWELVE**

"Oh," my mother said when she saw the police car in the parking lot of the animal shelter the next morning. A uniformed officer was talking to Kathy near the door to the animal wing. A second officer was talking to one of the shelter's maintenance people. Several of the other shelter staff members were standing around.

"I wonder what's going on," I said, reaching for the door handle.

"Robyn, wait," my mother said. She looked uncertainly at the police car. She was probably wondering if the police presence had anything to do with vicious dogs.

"There are animal control people who work here," I told her. "So if there was a problem with any of the animals here, they wouldn't call the police. They could handle it themselves."

My mother relaxed her grip on the steering wheel.

"You're probably right," she said. She looked at the two police officers again. "Be careful," she said.

I promised I would and got out of the car. After she left, I spotted Janet. I walked over to her.

"What happened?"

"There was a break-in."

"A break-in? What was taken? Was it the money from the mall displays?"

The question seemed to surprise her.

"That money has been in the bank for ages," she said. "And anyway, the break-in was in the animal wing, not the administrative wing. It happened on Saturday night."

"And the police only showed up *now?*" I said.

"The weekend staff discovered the broken lock on Sunday morning," Janet said. "They called Kathy. As far as anyone could tell, nothing was stolen. But you never know. So Kathy called the police. Since it was low priority and Kathy was up at her cottage, they said they'd send someone over first thing Monday morning to take the report."

"What do you mean, you never know?"

"Well, just because no one noticed anything missing, that doesn't mean that nothing was taken. This is a big shelter. Whoever broke in may have stolen something that no one has noticed yet. Kathy filed a report just in case. The insurance company will insist on it if she ever has to make a claim."

"Why would someone break in and not take any-thing?" I said. That didn't make sense.

Janet shrugged. "Maybe it was an animal rights ac-tivist trying to liberate some of the animals. They've staged a couple of protests here in the past when we've had to put an animal down."

"Were any animals released?"

Janet shook her head. "Maybe whoever broke in heard one of the weekend staff coming and got scared off before they could do anything. Or it could have been kids, just fooling around. Who knows?"

Finally, the police officer who had been talking to Kathy closed his notebook. He handed her something—a business card, I think—before walking back to his car. The other police officer joined him, and they drove away. Kathy waved at all of us to go inside.

I was outside later, eating lunch, when Kathy came out of the door to the animal wing and started back across the grass to the office. Ed Jarvis appeared around the side of the animal wing. He was leading the RAD group out onto the lawn with their dogs so that the dogs could run for a few minutes before they started their training session. I noticed that Nick and Orion weren't with them. I watched to see if they would appear from behind the building, but they didn't. Maybe Mr. Jarvis had given Nick something else to do.

Ed Jarvis spotted Kathy and called to her. She turned and waited for him to catch up to her.

"Can I talk to you for a minute?" he said. "It's about Nick."

They continued walking across the lawn. Suddenly Kathy stopped. Mr. Jarvis was doing most of the talking. Kathy listened. She started to shake her head. She looked so disappointed. But why?

Mr. Jarvis headed back to the RAD group and Kathy swung around and started walking back to the office. Behind her, I saw Antoine talking to Mr. Jarvis, gesturing with both hands. He broke away from the group and jogged after Kathy, trailing his dog behind him on a leash. He caught up with her not far from the picnic table where I was sitting.

"What about Nick's dog?" he said.

"What about him?" Kathy said.

"If you want me to, I can bring him out. You know, since Nick isn't here."

Kathy shook her head.

"Aw, come on," Antoine said. "The dog didn't do anything wrong."

Kathy shook her head again. "Orion isn't feeling well today."

Antoine frowned.

"What do you mean? Is he sick?"

"That's what I've been told."

"Really sick or just sort of sick?"

Even I wanted to hear the answer to that. But all Kathy said was, "He's sick, Antoine. And you have work to do." She nodded across the lawn to where all the RAD guys were lining up with their dogs. "You'd better get going." She turned and walked briskly back inside.

Antoine watched her for a moment. Then he led his dog back to where the others were waiting.

. . .

It was Janet who finally told me what Kathy had been shaking her head about.

"One of the RAD kids got arrested," she said.

"Nick?" I said. It had to be. He was the only one who was missing today. Janet nodded. "For breaking into the animal wing?"

Janet shook her head.

"I didn't get all the details," she said. "But it has something to do with a stolen car."

No wonder Kathy had looked so disappointed.

"Does that mean he won't be coming back?"

"I don't know," Janet said.

. . .

By mid-afternoon, my eyes were watering from staring at the computer screen. So I was glad when a flustered Janet poked her head into my office and asked if I could take someone over to the animal building.

"We're hiring for two animal care positions," she said. "Herb Leonard is doing the interviews. You know where his office is, right?"

I did. It was right near the dog kennels. After I had guided the way and introduced the candidate to Mr.

Leonard, I turned to retrace my steps. But instead of going right back to my office, I paused outside the kennels. Kathy had said that Orion was sick. I'm not sure why—maybe it was the picture I had of him leaning against Nick's thigh, quivering like jelly when Nick scratched behind his ear—but I wanted to see how he was.

The kennel area consisted of three wide aisles with dog kennels on each side. I walked down the first one, looking for Orion. He wasn't in there. When I turned the corner to go up the middle aisle, I passed a workman who was replacing a lock on the door that led out into the yard. He cursed loudly as he fiddled with it and then apologized when he noticed me.

I walked up the middle aisle, peeking into each kennel until I found the big black dog, flopped down on his blanket. It looked like he was sleeping, but he opened his eyes and raised his head a few millimeters when he heard me approach. Then he dropped his head back down again. His big, sad eyes fixed on me—I think he was disappointed to see me instead of Nick—and he *rowfed.* He didn't sound fierce at all.

"Poor dog," I murmured.

"Poor dog?" a voice said mockingly.

I whirled around. Antoine was standing behind me, holding a couple of folded blankets. He had his dog with him. It was straining on the leash that was wrapped around one of Antoine's wrists. Antoine tucked the blankets firmly under one arm and opened the door to a kennel on the other side of the aisle from Orion's.

"Easy, Jackie," he said as his dog started to bark and pull on its leash, yanking Antoine's arm away from the door. "Come, Jackie." He spoke in a calm, reassuring voice.

Jackie approached Antoine slowly.

"Good dog," Antoine said. He stepped into the kennel. "Come, Jackie."

The dog followed him inside. Antoine scooped up the blanket from the kennel floor and looked at me.

"You want to do something useful?" he said.

Before I could answer, he threw the blanket at me. While Antoine unfolded one of the clean blankets and laid it out on the floor for Jackie, I folded the old one and set it down on the floor. Antoine scratched the dog behind its ears and murmured something to him. It occurred to me then that Nick had been right, that Antoine had lashed out at the dog in frustration and that maybe it would never happen again. Watching him now, I could see that Antoine really liked the dog. He backed out of the kennel, closed the door, and slid the latch into place. He crossed to Orion's kennel.

"He didn't get out today," he said. "I offered, but—" He shrugged, unlatched the door to Orion's kennel and stepped inside. Orion didn't move. "Hey, boy, what's the matter?" Antoine said, crouching down. "You must be really sick. Either that or you miss Nick."

Antoine struggled to try to get Orion up off his blanket. When that didn't work, he wrestled the blanket out from under the big dog. He opened the kennel door and said, "Catch," as he tossed it to me. The door clicked shut again, and he spread a fresh blanket on the floor for Orion. This time Orion got to his feet, moved the few paces to the clean blanket, and flopped down onto it.

I stood outside the kennel with another armful of doggie blanket that smelled, well, like doggie. And, *eeew*, what was that sticky stuff on my hand? *Please don't let it be what I think it is.* I pulled my hand away from the blanket. Double-*eeew*. There was a smear of sticky brown stuff on my hand with, wait a minute—some sticky *blue* stuff. Dogs and sticky brown stuff—that was understandable. But dogs and sticky blue stuff didn't go together. I sniffed my hand cautiously. The good news was that whatever was on my hand wasn't what I had thought it was. It didn't smell bad. Not even remotely. And now that I was looking at it, I saw a different kind of brown stuff—crumbly brown stuff—mixed in with it. I wiped the stuff off on the blanket and made a note to wash my hands a few dozen times on my way back to my office.

Antoine gave Orion a good, long scratch behind the ears before coming out of the kennel and latching the door. He scooped up the dirty blanket I had dropped and reached for the one I was still holding. I gave it to him.

"What did Nick do?" I said.

Antoine stared at me with contemptuous eyes. "Looking for some good gossip?" he said. "Well, get it someplace else." He wheeled around and walked down the long corridor to the door, his sneakers silent on the tiled floor.

I stepped closer to Orion's cage and squatted down. He raised his head lethargically.

"Hey, Orion," I said softly.

Orion lay on his blanket at the back of his kennel and looked at me with his sad black eyes. Then, before I knew what was happening, he sprang to his feet and rushed the door. He jammed his nose through the chain-link and let loose a loud, furious roar. I was so startled that I screamed and fell backward, my heart pounding. Orion barked again and kept on barking. I scuttled backward on my hands and feet like a crab. He can't get out, I told myself. He can't hurt me. Then, over Orion's insistent bark, I heard another sound coming from the end of the aisle. I turned and saw Antoine, his hand on the door that led into the rest of the animal wing. He was laughing at me.

.   .   .

My mother phoned as I was shutting down my computer.

"Marlyse just called," she said. Marlyse Cosburn was a friend of my mother's. They'd met in law school. "She's referred a client to me. I won't be able to pick you up. And I haven't been able to reach your father."

"I thought Marlyse was on maternity leave," I said. The last time I'd seen her, Marlyse looked big enough to be carrying quintuplets.

"Exactly," my mother said.

"No problem," I said. "I'll take the bus."

"Meet me at the office, Robyn. I'll take you out to supper as soon as I'm through. We'll go to Vittorio's."

Vittorio's was my favorite Italian restaurant. It was on the same street as my mother's office.

"Sounds good," I said. "If I get there early, I'll go shopping. I need some new shoes."

I took the bus into the city and transferred to the subway. I still had some time to kill, so I wandered through a couple of stores. In one of them just two blocks from my mother's office, I found the perfect pair of sandals— except that they were one size too big.

"We're getting a new shipment in tomorrow," the clerk told me. "If you want, I can hold a pair for you."

"Great," I said. "I'll pick them up after I get off work."

A few minutes later, I was pushing open the front door to the converted Victorian house where my mother worked. Her office was on the second floor.

"Hey, Robyn," said Tralee White, one of the assistants, glancing up from her computer screen for a moment. "Long time, no see. Enjoying your summer?"

"It's okay," I said. "I'm supposed to meet my mother."

"She stepped out for a few minutes," Tralee said. Her printer began to spit out paper, which she retrieved and inserted into one of the file folders that were stacked on her desk. "She shouldn't be long. You can wait in her office if you'd like."

"I'm okay. I'll wait here."

I dropped down onto one of the comfy chairs in the reception area, picked up a magazine, and started to flip through it. Tralee reached for another file folder from the pile on her desk and let out a little cry of exasperation when the whole stack of them toppled to the floor.

"Should have seen that coming," she muttered.

I jumped to my feet to help her. A lot of the paper had slid out of the folders and lay strewn all over the floor. I had spent plenty of time at the office since my mother had started working there. It was practically a reflex to want to help. I started scooping up file folders while Tralee gathered their scattered contents. That's when I saw it—a name on a file label: D'ANGELO, Nicholas. Tralee put out a hand and I gave her the folder.

"What's going on?" said a voice from the doorway. My mother.

"Landslide," Tralee said. "Or should I say paperslide. Sorry, Patricia. I'll sort it all out before I leave."

My mother shook her head and joined us. Fifteen minutes later, we had everything more or less back in order. "Come on, Robyn," my mother said to me as she put the last file folder back onto Tralee's desk. "Ted is meeting us at the restaurant."

We walked to the restaurant and were shown to a table on the patio out back. We settled in, and my mother ordered a glass of wine while we waited for Ted. I ordered a Coke.

"Can I ask you something?" I said.

My mother looked at me.

"One of the file folders I picked up said Nick D'Angelo on it."

"Those were client files, Robyn."

"I didn't see anything that was in the file. I just saw his name."

"And?"

I hesitated. "And," I said slowly, "I know someone named Nick D'Angelo. He's in a special program at the animal shelter for kids who have been involved in violent offenses. He just got arrested."

My mother looked surprised. "You didn't tell me you knew any of the kids in that program."

"So it's the same Nick D'Angelo?"

My mother gave me the same look she'd given me after my first day at the shelter—it was a mixture of worry and concern. "You're not working with those kids, are you?" she said.

I shook my head. "I've talked to him a couple of times," I said. "Someone told me he stole a car."

"Who stole a car?" a voice behind me said. Ted. He smiled at me, kissed my mother on the cheek, and sat down.

"Mom's defending someone I know," I told Ted.

"Oh?" Ted said.

"He's one of Marlyse's clients," my mother said.

"And this friend of yours stole a car, Robyn?" Ted said. He glanced at my mother to gauge her reaction.

"He's not exactly a friend," I said.

There was that look again. "Actually," my mother said, "the charge is joyriding."

"Same thing," I said. "Joyriding means taking a car that doesn't belong to you. It's the same as stealing, right?"

I should have known better. Lawyers tend to be precise, especially when it comes to the law. If my mother had meant stealing, she would have said so.

"Stealing is when you take someone else's property with the intent to convert it to your own use either permanently or temporarily—when you take it to keep it or sell it and keep the money," my mother said. See what I mean? "When a person goes joyriding, he doesn't intend to keep the vehicle. It's like the difference between taking something and borrowing it."

"If you get a sympathetic cop, a sympathetic owner, or a sympathetic judge," Ted said, "you can usually get away with maybe a fine or a promise to work for the owner for a couple of Saturdays to pay for what you did."

My mother stared at him. "That sounds like the voice of experience, Ted."

Beneath his thinning blond hair, Ted's face turned crimson. "I grew up in a small farming community," he said, as if this were an explanation. But I didn't understand. Apparently neither did my mother. She crossed her arms over her chest.

"Everyone did it," Ted said.

"Great defense," my mother said.

"Tractors, mostly," Ted said. "Around Halloween, mostly. No harm done." He paused. "Mostly."

My mother's face was stern for, oh, about two seconds. Then the corners of her mouth twitched and she said, "One of the things I love about you is that you're full of surprises."

Love? I looked at her looking at Ted.

Ted beamed. "The point is," he said to me, "joyriding is a crime, but not a serious one."

"So what's the big deal?" I said.

"Ted's right," my mother said. "In and of itself, joyriding is a minor offense. Usually you get a fine, maybe community service, depending on what kind of trouble you've been in before."

Nick had been in plenty of trouble, as my mother undoubtedly knew.

"But," she said, looking directly at me, her face serious again, "this joyride included an accident."

"Accident?"

"The car hit a cyclist," my mother said.

I held my breath.

Ted shook his head. "Guns don't kill people—people kill people," he said.

"The *driver* of the car hit a cyclist," my mother amended. "Knocked the poor man right off his bike and then didn't stop or remain at the scene. Fortunately, the injuries aren't life-threatening."

Thank goodness for that.

"So it's not that serious?" I said.

My mother gave me a sharp look. "The charges are very serious," she said. "First of all, taking a car that doesn't belong to you without the owner's permission is an offense. So is driving without a license. Second, the cyclist broke his collarbone and a couple of ribs. So this boy is looking at criminal negligence—another offense. Third, the law requires drivers to stop when they are involved in an accident, to remain at the scene until the police arrive, and to offer assistance to any injured parties. An adult who doesn't stop can land in jail for up to five years. Finally, all of this happened while the boy was living in a group home as a result of a previous charge. He was given leave for the weekend on condition that he stay with his aunt at all times, which he failed to do. I can't even begin to imagine what was going through his head. He had less than three months left at the group home before he could go and live with his aunt permanently. He's thrown that away."

"He's living in a group home?" Ted said. "Where are his parents?"

My mother hesitated for a moment. "You're not to repeat any of this," she said finally, looking at me, even though it was Ted who had asked the question. "According to Marlyse, this boy is a textbook case. Unstable home life from an early age. Neglect. Probably physical abuse—you should see his file. He'd show up to school with all kinds of bruises and injuries, but his mother always denied that anything was going on. He was still underage when he started getting into trouble—little things at first, acting out, you know, shoplifting, petty theft. Then, sure enough, school yard fights—lots of them. He's a boy with a lot of problems, Robyn." It sounded as if she was warning me. "The only real surprise is that this time he didn't try to deny what he'd done."

"He didn't?" I said.

"He's pleading guilty."

"Then why does he need a lawyer?"

"I'm representing him, not defending him," my mother said. "He's a youth. My job is to make sure he understands what he's doing and that he gets the best disposition for someone in his situation."

"What do you think will happen, Mom?"

She said *if* Nick were lucky and *if* he had an explanation for what he had done and *if* the judge believed that he hadn't stopped because he was scared and that he was now very sorry and *if* he could gather enough character witnesses who would say good things about him, assuming such witnesses existed, he might get another open custody disposition, maybe six months or a year. She said that would be pretty good. She said if he were an adult with the same record of offenses, a judge could be harsh and he could end up with a couple of years in prison. Then she said, "Exactly how well do you know this boy, Robyn?"

"Not very well," I said. Which was true. A few days ago, I thought I had Nick figured out, but now that he was living up—or was it down?—to my original expectations, I wasn't sure.

CHAPTER **THIRTEEN**

"**L**et me get this straight," Morgan said when she called me that night. "Your mother is defending the guy who stole the money from our pet pageant in junior high?"

"She's representing him," I said. "But it's not for stealing money. It's for joyriding and leaving the scene of an accident."

"Boy, you must be really mad," Morgan said.

Huh?

"Why would I be mad?"

"Come on," Morgan said. "It drove you crazy when he took that money and spent it on something stupid. What did he do with it again?"

"Treated a bunch of kids to a night at the arcade," I said. Morgan was right. It had really bothered me. We had worked for weeks to organize the pet pageant to benefit a good cause, and Nick had blown the money in one night and had ended up with nothing to show for it. "But that has nothing to do with this."

"Of course it does," Morgan said. "You have a history with him. You caught him stealing—twice. Now he's in trouble again—big trouble. And whom does he get for a lawyer? Your mother. Perfectionist Patti, the lawyer with the double A-type personality. She'll get him off for sure. And you're going to tell me that won't bother you?"

"First of all," I said, "if my mother ever hears you refer to her that way, she'll bar you from the house. Permanently. Second, I already told you, she's not *defending* him. He admitted he did it. He's pleading guilty. She's just representing him on sentencing."

"Oh," Morgan said, sounding a little deflated. "So now when Nick D'Angelo messes up, he fesses up, is that it?"

"Yeah, I guess," I said. That had been bothering me ever since my mother had told me.

"What?" Morgan said.

"What do you mean, what?"

"Something's bugging you. I can hear it in your voice. Come on. Tell me. What's going on?"

"Nothing," I said. But that wasn't true. "It's just that, well, people at the animal shelter like him. Apparently he's doing really well there. He's a sort of role model for the other kids in the RAD program. He looks out for some of them too. He knows a lot about dogs. He even volunteers at the shelter one day a week when he's not there for RAD. And there's this dog—Nick has been working with him. I heard him ask if he could adopt him."

"Yeah?" Morgan said. "So?"

"So . . ." I wished I knew, but I didn't. "So nothing, I guess."

There was a pause on the other end of the line. Then Morgan said, "You like him, don't you?"

"No!"

"Uh-huh." She didn't believe me. "Either you have a dark side that I don't know about, or he's incredibly hot. And since I've known you practically your whole life, I'm going with hot. Am I right?"

"Well . . ."

"I knew it," Morgan said, sounding insufferably smug. "What does he look like?"

I told her. She sighed.

"What a waste," she said. "Majorly cute and behind bars."

"Yeah, but . . ."

"But what?" Morgan said.

But . . . I felt the same way my mother did. I could not understand why someone who was so close to being able to get out of his group home, and who cared about Orion so much, would throw it all away by doing something as phenomenally stupid as taking a car and going joyriding. He didn't even have a driver's license. What kind of sense did that make?

When I explained it to Morgan, all she said was "I bet if you ask your dad, he'll tell you that most people who get into trouble with the law aren't criminal master-minds. I bet he'll tell you the opposite is true—they're people who *don't* think before they act. Come on, Robyn. You said he's in that program at the animal shelter because he was charged with a violent offense. He has a history of not thinking. What's not to understand?"

She was probably right.

Except that she hadn't seen what I had seen. She hadn't heard Nick's voice as he pleaded with Kathy to let him adopt Orion or, at least, to let his aunt adopt the dog. She hadn't seen Nick sneak gourmet dog biscuits to Orion or heard Nick beg me not to tell on Antoine. I had.

On the other hand, nor had she seen Nick dart out of the school office four years ago with the money Morgan and Billy and I had worked so hard to raise. She hadn't seen him offer a resentful apology to Mr. Schuster only because he'd been forced to. She hadn't heard the sneer in his voice when he told me I had nothing on him after someone touched the fund-raising money.

"Take my advice," Morgan said. "Forget about him. Hey, one more week and I'll be home again. We can go back-to-school shopping."

. . .

When my mother dropped me off at the animal shelter the next morning, she pressed some money into my hand.

"What's that for?" I said.

"Bus fare," she said. "I won't be able to pick you up today, either. Your father's tied up today too. I could ask Ted—"

"The bus is fine, Mom. It's not a problem, really."

That afternoon, Kathy and I sat opposite each other at her desk with a couple of boxes of thank-you cards and envelopes between us. Volunteers had spent all the previous day addressing the envelopes by hand. Now Kathy was going to personally sign each card, and I was going to put the cards into envelopes and seal them.

"The personal touch," Kathy said. "It's supposed to make people feel good about giving to us, and that's supposed to translate into bigger donations. Heaven knows we could use the money."

"I never realized how much fund-raising went on in an animal shelter," I said.

She sighed. "It used to be relatively easy to get government funding," she said. "But that's not true anymore. I've been sending grant proposals to all the private foundations I can think of." I remembered the proposal that I had couriered out for her on Friday. "We have more animals here than we're designed to hold. We're managing to get most of them adopted, but it takes time. And the more animals we have here, the more we have to spend on food for them and on keeping them clean and healthy. That's why we're doing this." She nodded at the stack of cards that she was signing. "The only way we can keep all these animals alive is if we have enough money to look after them while we try to find them new homes. I told the staff yesterday. Now I'm telling the volunteers."

I looked apprehensively at her. Telling us what?

"We don't like to put animals down," she said. "We have to do it sometimes when an animal poses a genuine threat to people or other animals. But we only have so much space, so sometimes we also have to consider it when an animal is unlikely to be adopted because of its age or temperament or when our shelter and other shelters are overcrowded and there is no chance of early relief." She sighed again. "I found out on Friday that the government turned down our request for more funding. Over the weekend, our board of directors had to make a decision. For the time being, they've decided to impose a strict limit on how long an animal can stay here before we have to either get it adopted or find another home for it. After that . . ." She shook her head.

Someone knocked on the door. Before I could turn around, Kathy said, "What is it, Antoine?"

Antoine gave me a hard look before saying to Kathy, "Can I ask you something?"

"Shoot," Kathy said.

"Alone?"

"I'm racing the clock here, Antoine," Kathy said. "I need to get all of these cards signed, sealed, and into the mail today. You can ask your question right now while Robyn and I get this done, or you can wait until Thursday. Your choice."

I stuffed a card into an envelope and sealed it. Out of the corner of my eye I saw Antoine struggling to decide.

Finally, he said, "I was wondering if you're going to assign Orion to someone else, you know, in case Nick doesn't come back."

Kathy scrawled her signature on a card, pushed it across the table to me, and drew another one from the box in front of her. She didn't even look up as she said, "Nick is responsible for Orion, and Nick isn't here."

"Maybe I could look after him," Antoine said. "You know, for Nick."

Kathy was shaking her head before he finished speaking. "You've got your hands full," she said. "So do the others."

"Yeah, but Orion—"

"You know the rules, Antoine. These are last-chance dogs. When you and Nick and the others joined the program, you agreed to be paired with an animal and to take full responsibility for that animal. It's up to you guys to show up, to put your best effort into the program, and to do whatever you can to help these dogs become adoptable."

"I heard Stella say that Orion is making real progress," Antoine said.

"He is," Kathy said. "But this is a demonstration program. We explained to you what that meant. It's been designed to run a certain length of time in a certain way to meet certain objectives. When it's finished, it's going to be evaluated. If it gets a good evaluation, we might be able to get more funding and to persuade other shelters to set up programs like it. Nick knows that too, just like he knows that Orion depends on him to—" She broke off abruptly. When she spoke again, her voice was calmer. "If you or Nick or anyone else wants to know what's going to happen with Orion, you should look at the agreement you signed when you joined RAD. Do you remember that agreement, Antoine?" Antoine looked blank. Maybe he hadn't read his copy carefully before he signed it. "The program is a partnership between the youth participant and the canine participant. If the youth participant drops out for any reason, the canine participant can't continue."

"So are you saying that Orion won't be able to stay in the program?"

"That's exactly what I'm saying," Kathy said. Her phone rang. She picked it up, listened for a few seconds, and said, "Just a moment." She looked at Antoine. "You'd better get to your session," she said. "And, Robyn, can you give me a few minutes? I have to take this call."

Antoine was halfway down the hall by the time I caught up with him.

"Have you seen him?" I said. "Nick, I mean."

Antoine eyed me suspiciously.

"Why do you want to know?" he said.

"Because—" Because why? I wasn't even sure. "Because I don't think it's fair that Orion has to pay for something that Nick did."

That's when Antoine surprised me. He said, "I'd hate it if Jackie was stuck here forever because I messed up. Man, you should have heard Orion barking when the rest of the guys went in to get their dogs. That's why I volunteered to take care of him until Nick comes back."

If he comes back, I thought.

Antoine looked at me. "Nick said it was nice of you to go and see Orion, especially considering how scared you are of him. Of Orion, I mean."

"So you have seen him?"

"We live in the same place."

Oh.

"Are you going to tell him what Kathy said?"

He looked down at the ground.

"There are too many animals here, Antoine. The shelter has a new rule. If an animal can't be adopted after a certain amount of time, they're going to put it down."

"*What?*" He stared at me, stunned. "Since when? Who told you?"

"Kathy did. Just before you showed up."

"They can't do that!"

"They have to."

Antoine looked like he couldn't believe it. "I told Nick I'd talk to Kathy, you know, to make sure Orion was going to be okay," he said finally. "But after what she said and after what you just told me, I'm thinking maybe I'll tell him that she wasn't around today."

"You mean you're going to lie to him?"

Antoine bristled at that. "He's my friend."

"So maybe you should tell him the truth."

"You know, Nick's right. You're a real pain!"

"He said that?"

"He told me how you got him busted a few years back. He told me you were a real brownnoser back then, and that you haven't changed much. He said you tried to get him in trouble with Kathy."

"I thought he took some money," I said.

"Yeah, well, he didn't. Nick's not like that."

"I saw him do it before."

"That's your story."

"His is different?"

Antoine just shrugged.

"He took a car that didn't belong to him," I said.

"Says you," he said. "Says the cops."

"Says Nick," I said. "He's not denying it, Antoine. He said he did it."

Antoine's face darkened. This was obviously news to him. "How do you know?"

I didn't want to bring my mother into it. Antoine would probably stop talking to me if he knew she was Nick's lawyer. So instead I said, "Didn't he tell you?"

"He hasn't told me anything." He shook his head, as if he were struggling to absorb what I had just told him. "I only got to see him for a few minutes. He asked me to talk to Kathy." He shook his head again. "No way would Nick take a car. He says doing stuff like that is stupid. He tells me that all the time."

He sounded so positive. It had to mean something that even Antoine couldn't understand why Nick would give up so much—the chance to finally leave the group home, the chance to live with his aunt and, maybe, Orion—to do something as stupid as go joyriding.

"What are you going to do, Antoine?" I said.

"Am I going to tell him that if he doesn't come back, Orion doesn't get to be in the program anymore? That he might get put down?" He shook his head firmly. "I didn't even tell him that Orion was sick. He'd freak out. He's crazy about that dog. And he's got enough to worry about already, you know?"

. . .

I went downtown after work to pick up my new sandals. After I paid for them, I called my mother's office. I thought that if she were finished for the day, we could go home together.

"She's in a meeting," Tralee told me. "But she should be out pretty soon."

"Tell her not to leave without me," I said.

As soon as I turned the corner to the street where my mother works, I stopped dead in my tracks. Nick was standing on the sidewalk outside of her office. As usual, he was dressed in black from head to toe, and as usual, his backpack hung off one shoulder. His friend Joey was with him. Nick glanced in my direction. I know he saw me, but he turned away as if he hadn't. Joey saw me too, but he didn't try to hide it. He gave me a critical once-over before dismissing me. I walked toward them.

"I saw Orion today," I said to Nick.

He didn't say anything. He didn't even look at me. Instead, he focused on the ground.

"I don't know if anyone told you," I said. I knew Antoine hadn't. "But he's been sick."

That got a reaction. Nick's head bobbed up. He glanced at Joey. If I didn't know better, I'd say he looked angry. "He's going to be okay, right?" he said.

It was a funny question. If I was as fond of a dog as Nick was of Orion and someone told me that the dog had been sick, the first thing I would have asked was what exactly was wrong with him or how had he gotten sick.

"I don't know," I said. "All I know is that he was really sick on Sunday. Yesterday, too. They think maybe he caught something." I had talked to one of the kennel attendants, who reminded me that there had been a virus going around. "He was feeling a little better today, except that Antoine told me he was barking like crazy when all the other dogs got out for the program today and he had to stay in his kennel."

Hurt flickered in Nick's eyes. I think Joey noticed.

"Why don't you take off, little girl?" Joey said.

I ignored him.

"Kathy says if you don't come back to the shelter, Orion won't be able to finish the program," I said. "And if he doesn't finish the program, he can't be adopted."

"That's not fair," Nick said. "Orion is doing great. Kathy would never let anything happen to him. Besides, my lawyer's going to fix it so I can stay with the program. And the wheels of justice don't turn as fast as they make you think on TV." He glanced at Joey, who nodded. "My court date is a couple of weeks away. That will give me time to finish the program. Orion will be okay. Anyway, my lawyer said it would look good when I go to court if I could show that I'd done the program."

I couldn't believe it. He was acting as if nothing serious had happened, as if he hadn't done anything wrong, and as if, of course, he'd be allowed to go back. He didn't seem even remotely concerned about the poor man he'd knocked off his bike.

"You hit someone," I said.

Finally. He flinched. For a split second I thought I saw pain and regret in his eyes, maybe even remorse. He glanced at Joey again.

"The guy walked away," Nick said. "How bad could it be?"

"Hey, Nick, you don't want to be talking about this with anyone," Joey said. "The less you say, the better. Right?"

The *less* he said? He had already been caught. He had admitted he'd done it.

"Yeah, I guess," Nick said. He looked defiantly at me.

That did it. That made me mad.

"You're too much," I said. "You put everything you have into helping a dog, but there's a man in the hospital because of what you did, and you don't even care. Antoine tried to tell me you're okay. He said you're always telling him not to do anything stupid. But look at what you did! And you think it's all a big joke."

Joey stepped between Nick and me. He moved in close and kept coming, trying to back me away from Nick.

"Why don't you mind your own business?" he said.

Nick grabbed him by the arm and yanked him away.

"Leave her alone," he said. He sounded angry—with Joey, not with me. He looked at me, his eyes not nearly as hard as they had been a moment ago.

"I'm sorry about the guy," he said. "But he's going to be okay."

"Nick!" an angry voice called.

All three of us turned. A woman was standing in the door to my mother's office building, her hands on her hips, glowering disapproval at him. It was the same woman who picked him up every day from the animal shelter. Nick shot a worried look at Joey. Joey shrugged, like it was no big deal. He walked away, just like that, without a word.

"Are you *trying* to make things harder on yourself, Nick?" the woman said. "I trust you to go to the restroom and what happens? You leave the building. And then I find you out here with Joey." She shook her head.

"He just showed up," Nick said. "My aunt must have told him I was seeing my lawyer."

The woman was as stern as a school principal. "Your aunt wouldn't do that, Nick. Your aunt wants you to stay out of trouble, not get into more of it. I know you're not allowed to receive calls from Joey. Did you phone him, Nick? Because I can't think of any other way that he'd be here, can you?" Of course Nick didn't answer.

"About the RAD program," Nick said. "Did my lawyer fix it? Am I still in?"

"That depends. Am I going to see Joey around again anytime soon?"

"Never. I promise," Nick said. He sounded like a little kid now. Please, please, please.

"You were ordered to do an anger management program," the woman said. "So, yes, you're still in RAD. But only until a judge says differently and only if you follow the rules. You got that?" Nick nodded. "Okay. Let's go."

.   .   .

Maybe Nick was allowed to stay in RAD, but he must not have been allowed out otherwise. He didn't show up at the shelter the next day for his once-a-week Wednesday volunteering. I didn't see him again until Thursday when he arrived with Antoine and Dougie and the rest of the RAD guys. They all took their dogs outside for ten or fifteen minutes. Nick brought Orion to one side of the fenced-in lawn they started to practice what they had been learning. Nick had Orion sit, lie down, sit again, and then shake a paw. It looked like Orion hadn't forgotten a thing while he was gone. Nick smiled, dropped down on his knees, and scratched behind the dog's ears.

Then he put his arms around Orion and hugged him. He adored that dog. I still couldn't figure out how he could be so attached to an animal and, at the same time, not seem to care at all about someone he had injured.

"Robyn?"

I tore my eyes away from the window. Kathy stood in the door to my office, her face flushed. She was dressed more formally than usual, in a skirt and light jacket.

"Go and tell Mr. Jarvis and Stella they can get started. We'll be around in a few minutes. And tell them not to let the guys know what's going on, okay? I want everyone to act the way they would if this were a regular day."

But it wasn't a regular day. It was a big day. The chairman of the shelter's board of directors had called Kathy at home that morning. He'd said that he was bringing some visitors to observe the RAD program in action. Apparently, there was a possibility that these visitors might fund the program so that it could continue. Kathy wanted everything to be perfect. All morning, shelter staff had been running around, tidying up, and making sure that everything sparkled. Kathy was especially eager. She wanted the visitors to understand how the program helped both the kids and the dogs. She also wanted to talk to them about expanding the program to other shelters. It was, she said, the best opportunity she'd had in a long time.

The visitors had arrived thirty minutes ago, and Kathy had been showing them around. I could see them over her shoulder—two men in suits (one of them the chairman of the shelter's board of directors) and a woman in a summer dress. They were in the office across the hall from mine, watching a video of the RAD participants and their dogs on the first day of the program. Kathy had showed me the video while she was setting up earlier. She said it would make a big impression because, in it, the dogs all barked and jumped up on people and generally misbehaved. A lot of the RAD participants looked uncomfortable. One of them—Dougie—looked terrified. They had no idea how to control the rambunctious dogs. The plan was that the visitors would watch the video—the "before"—and then go outside, watch the RAD group in action and see the "after."

I hurried outside to deliver Kathy's message. Mr. Jarvis looked as tense as Kathy. He wanted the program to continue too. He whispered something in Stella's ear, and she called for the group's attention. The RAD participants and their animals lined up in front of her. A door to the field opened, and Kathy came out, leading the visitors. Stella nodded to Nick, who was at the beginning of the line of RAD participants.

"Why don't you run Orion through everything he's learned so far?" she said.

Nick seemed delighted to do so. First, he got Orion to sit. Then he got him to lie down. As the visitors approached, Orion extended a paw for Nick to shake. Kathy was beaming. The visitors were standing with the boys and the dogs. One of them said something to Nick. Nick grinned and said something to the woman visitor and she nodded. Orion sat again and extended a paw. The woman took it and shook it. She smiled first at the dog and then at Nick. Then she smiled at the male visitor. I had a pretty good idea what was going through their minds. After viewing the video of the first day of the program, they couldn't help but be impressed by what they were seeing. Kathy was talking the whole time. I glanced at Mr. Jarvis. He seemed more relaxed now too. It looked like everything was going as smoothly as Kathy had planned.

Then it all went wrong.

CHAPTER **FOURTEEN**

Janet was leading two uniformed police officers across the lawn toward the RAD group. When Kathy saw them, she excused herself and hurried over to speak with them. I watched her shoulders slump as she listened to what they said. She turned and gestured at the RAD group. The two police officers walked across the lawn to Nick. One of them touched him on the shoulder. While the first cop said something to Nick, the second one pulled Nick's hands behind his back to handcuff him. Orion went crazy. I took a big step back—an automatic reflex. He barked ferociously and jumped up on the police officer who was trying to handcuff Nick. The rest of the RAD group just stood there, watching. Stella, the dog trainer, stepped forward, but Nick shook his head. He said something to the two cops. The one who was holding him let him go. Nick got Orion to stop barking. He made him sit and stay. Then he let himself be handcuffed. I saw Nick's face clearly when he turned around. He seemed dazed. The chairman of the shelter's board of directors did not look pleased. The police officer who had handcuffed Nick touched him on the shoulder again and nodded toward the police car in the parking lot. When Nick began to walk toward it, Orion sprang to his feet and started barking again. This time Stella took him by the collar and got him to sit. But she couldn't make him stop barking. As the police led Nick past me, I heard him say, "This wasn't supposed to happen." He looked over his shoulder at the big dog. I'd never seen anyone look so sad or so lost.

Kathy put on a brave face. She continued to smile, but I could see that the spark had vanished from her eyes. The discipline of the RAD group fell apart. The guys watched the police put Nick into the back of a patrol car and talked among themselves. Even Mr. Jarvis watched Nick for a few moments before clapping his hands to bring the group back to order. The chairman of the shelter's board of directors was talking to the two visitors, but their eyes kept shifting back to the police car. They didn't stay for long after that.

I went back to my office and called my mother.

"I'm just on my way out, Robyn," she said. "Is this important?"

"The police were just here, Mom. They arrested Nick."

"I know," she said. "I'm on my way to the police station."

"But what happened? Why did they arrest him again?"

There was a brief pause on the other end of the phone before my mother said, "The man died."

No wonder Nick had looked so dazed.

"But you said his injuries weren't life threatening," I said.

"They weren't. But the man had a preexisting condition. The trauma of the hit-and-run triggered a heart attack. At least, that's what they're saying."

"But that's not Nick's fault," I said.

"He was driving that car, Robyn. He hit the man."

"But—"

"Robyn, I have to go. I'll see you at home later, okay?"

I sat silent at my desk for a few moments after I hung up. Then the shouting began. I think everyone in the shelter heard it.

"A killer!" said an angry voice—the chairman of the animal shelter's board of directors. "You have a killer in this program, and you didn't think to alert me to that fact?"

"You make it sound worse than it is, Harold," Kathy said.

"The boy hit someone with a car," Harold said. "A *stolen* car. Now that person is dead. Criminal negligence causing death—isn't that what the police officer said?"

"The person—the victim—" Kathy seemed to say the word only reluctantly, "was injured in the accident, but—"

"He died," Harold said again. "If the authorities didn't think his death was related to the hit-and-run, they wouldn't have charged the boy. And of all things, to have the police show up when the Archers were here for their tour!"

"I'm sorry," Kathy said. "But I had no idea that was going to happen—"

Harold cut her off. "That boy doesn't belong in the program. He is not to return under any circumstances. Do you understand?"

"But he's made such progress," Kathy said. "And he's essentially a good kid. He does reasonably well in school, according to Ed Jarvis. He's seen as a leader of sorts among the other boys at his group home. He has a part-time job. And he's been volunteering here for—"

"He *volunteers* here?"

"One day a week," Kathy said.

"Not anymore," the chairman. "He's out of the RAD program and out of the volunteer program. Do you understand?"

. . .

My mother didn't pick me up that day—no surprise. Instead, my father was waiting for me in the parking lot. As I crossed the lawn toward him, I spotted something half-hidden behind one of the shrubs that lined the building. It was a backpack. I would have recognized it anywhere. It was Nick's. He always had it slung over

172

one shoulder. He must have forgotten about it when he was arrested. I scooped it up. At first I was going to run back inside and give it to Kathy. She could give it to Mr. Jarvis, and he would see that it was returned to Nick. Then I thought, no, I'll give it to my mother instead. She can get it directly to Nick. I scooped it up and took it with me to my father's car.

On the way home, I kept thinking about Nick looking back at Orion while he was being led away by the police. He was probably worried about what would happen to Orion now. When we finally got upstairs, my father tossed his jacket onto the closest chair and flopped down on a couch.

"What's up, Robbie?" he said. "And don't tell me nothing. I've known you your whole life. I can tell the happy, everything's-coming-up-roses Robbie from the unhappy, something's-definitely-wrong Robbie."

I sank down into a chair opposite him. "It's Nick," I said.

"The kid at the shelter whom you're not interested in?"

I nodded.

"What about him?"

"He was arrested."

"Oh?"

I told my father everything that had happened. When I had finished, he said, "I'm not sure I understand. You had him pegged as a thief, but you're surprised that he went joyriding?"

I knew it didn't make sense to him. It didn't make sense to me, either. That was the problem.

"I heard Kathy tell him he was doing well in the RAD program," I said. "And he loves that dog. He was trying to talk his aunt into adopting him. He was counting the days until he could get out of that group home and go live with his aunt. So why, when he finally gets a chance to get out for a weekend, would he do something so stupid?"

"Oh, I see," my father said. "You want logical. You want to know the number one thing I learned while I was a police officer?"

Even if I didn't, I was pretty sure he was going to tell me.

"People don't always act logically," he said. "I once arrested a guy who had never done anything wrong, never even collected a parking ticket. When he found a wallet on the sidewalk stuffed with hundred-dollar bills, he returned it to the owner just like that, didn't even accept a reward."

"What did you arrest him for?"

"For taking a baseball bat and smashing every window in his neighbor's car. And after he'd totaled the windows, he started in on the hood, the trunk, the doors. Dimpled the whole car—with the neighbor watching. He even knew that the neighbor had called the police."

"Why would someone who was so law-abiding do something like that?"

"The guy with the baseball bat suffered from insomnia. The neighbor worked nights as a bartender. His car needed a new muffler. He would pull into the driveway at two or three in the morning with his engine roaring. The guy had talked to him a couple of times. He'd even filed a complaint, and the neighbor was cited. But the neighbor didn't fix the muffler. Meanwhile, the guy's insomnia was getting worse and worse. Finally, he couldn't take it anymore. He snapped. Decided to deal with the car himself. Not logical, maybe. But it was the end of the muffler problem."

"What does that have to do with Nick?"

"Maybe there are other things going on in his life. Things you don't know about."

"Maybe," I said.

My father was probably right. Maybe Nick was like Antoine. Maybe he did stupid things for stupid reasons. Maybe something had happened while he was staying with his aunt on the weekend, and maybe, because of that, he had acted impulsively.

"Tell you what, Robbie, when I get a chance, I'll talk to someone on the force. I'll see what he can find out. Okay?"

My phone rang. It was my mother. I listened to what she had to say. Then I told my father, "Looks like I'm staying the night."

"Is everything okay?"

"She has to work late, and she has an early court date. She says you're going to have to drive me to the shelter, so I might as well stay here."

"Do you have everything you need, or do you want me to run you home?"

"I'll be okay," I said. "I've got some clean clothes here."

Halfway through dinner, my phone rang again. This time it was Morgan. I took my phone into the bedroom that my father calls mine, but that also doubles as his guest room. My purse and Nick's backpack were on the bed where I had dropped them after my mother called.

"Three more days," Morgan said. "I'll be home Sunday night."

"Nick got arrested *again*," I said. "The man he hit died."

"You're kidding!"

"They're charging him with criminal negligence causing death."

"He just goes from bad to worse, huh?"

"I still don't get it, Morgan. It was such a stupid thing to do."

"Come on, Robyn, you think that just because Nick D'Angelo makes nice to a dog, he's all of a sudden a good guy? There's a reason he's in that program, isn't there?" She sounded just like my father. And just like my father, she was right. "You don't even know what he did to get locked up in the first place, other than it was a violent crime," she went on. "Maybe he ran over someone else. Maybe he's a serial hit-and-runner, and you just don't know it. Why don't you ask your mom? She'd know."

But would she tell me? I glanced at my bed.

"He carries a backpack with him all the time," I said slowly. "You know, like some girls always carry a purse."

"Yeah?" Morgan said. "So?"

"So I have it."

There was a small pause. Then Morgan said, "You have Nick D'Angelo's backpack? What did you do, steal it?"

"Of course not," I said indignantly. "He forgot to take it when he got arrested. I'm going to give it to my mother so that she can give it back to him."

"Is there anything interesting in it?" Morgan said.

"I don't know."

"You mean you haven't looked?"

"No!"

"But you're going to, right?"

"No, I'm not!" I said. Except I wasn't sure that was true. I was dying to look, and Morgan probably knew it.

"Open it," she said.

"I don't know—"

"Sure you do, Robyn. That's why you brought it up in the first place. You want to see what's inside, and you want someone to give you permission to look. *I* give you permission. Besides, who's going to know?"

"I will."

"So will I. But I won't tell. Come on, open it up. Tell me what's inside."

I stared at my bed again and at the backpack on it. How would I feel if Nick picked up my purse and went through all the personal stuff I kept in it?

"I really shouldn't."

"Sure you should," Morgan said. "You keep telling me that you don't understand him. Well, here's your chance to get some insight. Go ahead, open it up."

I started to drag it toward me. Then I stopped. It was Nick's private property. It wouldn't be right to poke through it.

"Don't be such a wuss, Robyn," Morgan said. "It's not like you're going to take anything. You're just going to satisfy your curiosity."

I stared at the backpack and thought about Nick with his purple-blue eyes and the scar that cut across his right cheek. Nick, who dressed all in black and who worked hard at trying to make people think he didn't care about anything. But he never quite pulled it off. He cared about Orion. He'd sounded like a little boy when he'd begged Kathy to let him take Orion home for the weekend. He cared about the guys in his group. He had even cared about that little girl who he introduced to Orion. What did a guy like that carry around with him every day?

"Okay, I'm unzipping it now," I said.

"Way to go, Robyn."

I glanced at the door, half afraid that my dad would walk in and see what I was doing. But he hadn't even mentioned the backpack. He probably assumed it was mine.

I peeked inside.

"Well?" Morgan said.

"I see a big book." I pulled it out. It was the book he had been reading the time we'd had lunch together. "It's all about dogs." Everything you need to know about them, according to the title. "Also a notebook." I flipped through it. Nick's handwriting was small and scratchy, but I managed to decipher it. "Looks like notes that he took from the book and stuff that he's learned about dogs from the RAD program," I said.

"What else?"

I pulled out more items. "A pack of gum." Two pieces were missing. "A rawhide bone and . . . *Eeew!* What are these?" I held up a clear-plastic package and read the label. "Dried pigs' ears! Gross."

"Dogs love those," Morgan said. "Missy would eat pigs' ears morning, noon, and night if I let her." Missy was Morgan's black Lab. "What else?"

"A pair of socks." They were rolled in a ball and smelled clean. "Something in wrapping paper." The paper was covered with balloons and cakes with candles on them and was loosely wrapped around a brand-new dog collar. I told Morgan about it and went on, "An apple, slightly bruised but still edible, and a can of warm Coke."

"That's it?" Morgan sounded disappointed. "Did you check all the pockets?"

I hadn't. I told myself I shouldn't. But I felt around anyway. There was something in a small zippered pocket. I pulled it out.

"Oh," I said.

"What?" Morgan said. "Did you find something?"

I stared at the small slips of paper that had been clipped together.

"What is it?" Morgan said. "What did you find?"

"Transaction slips," I said. "From an ATM. You know, printouts of recent activity from a bank account. Six of them," I counted, "going back—" I checked, "about six months."

"And?"

I skimmed the slips. There were regular deposits of fifty dollars a week, week in and week out, for over a year—and regular, much smaller withdrawals. It seemed like a lot of allowance money for a kid in a group home. Then I remembered Kathy saying that Nick had a part-time job. I looked at the transaction slips again. Two weeks ago, the balance had been over fifteen hundred dollars. Ten days ago, it dropped to less than five hundred dollars. Suddenly I felt terrible.

"I'm putting everything back, Morgan. This is wrong."

"Are you thinking what I'm thinking, Robyn?"

Nick had withdrawn a lot of money—just before I saw him pressing a wad of bills through the fence to his friend Joey.

"Maybe he didn't give Joey stolen money," Morgan said. "Maybe he gave him his own money."

Oh, this was so wrong.

"I gotta go, Morgan," I said.

"You didn't take anything, Robyn. You didn't do anything bad. You were just looking."

"I'll call you soon," I said.

I closed my phone and started putting everything back exactly as I had found it. The big dog book was the last thing to go in. I opened it before returning it to the backpack. There was Nick's name, in big black letters and, under it, an inscription: *To Nick, a dog's best friend, from Stella*. Stella, the dog trainer. She had dated her inscription. She had given the book to Nick over three weeks ago. And judging from how much highlighting he'd done, he had been studying the contents carefully. In the section called "Caring for Your Dog," he had put little check marks beside the recommended basic dog care equipment and had underlined what to feed dogs—and what to avoid feeding them.

When I set the book back into the backpack, I noticed something I hadn't seen the first time. A squarish envelope, the kind that might hold a greeting card. I hesitated. I'd already gone through everything else. Why not go all the way?

I pulled out the envelope and opened it. I was right. It held a greeting card—a funny birthday card. There were two photographs inside. One was old. It was a picture of Nick as I remembered him from junior high. There was another, older boy in the picture with him. They were both grinning at the camera. A sticky note on the back said, "Found this. Thought you'd like it." The second photograph was more recent—Nick in the middle, his arms around the people on either side of him, Joey and a young woman in a waitress uniform who looked vaguely familiar. No wonder. The card was signed *Angie*.

CHAPTER **FIFTEEN**

As soon as I settled down at my computer the next day, two things happened. First, I realized that I'd left Nick's backpack at my father's place. I had felt so guilty after snooping in it that I'd put it in the closet where I couldn't see it. I would have to pick it up before I could give it to my mother to return to Nick.

Second, I saw Mr. Schuster. He was out on the lawn with Orion, running the big dog through everything he had learned in the RAD program. When he finished, he turned him free for a run. By the time my morning break rolled around, Mr. Schuster was sitting at the picnic table and Orion was lying at his feet. I went outside to say hi. Orion jumped up when he saw me. That stopped me in my tracks. Mr. Schuster settled him. I approached more cautiously, giving Orion a wide berth.

Mr. Schuster looked healthy and rested.

"I'm glad you're feeling better," I said.

"I guess I gave everyone a good scare," he said. "Scared myself too. When you get to be my age and you black out like that, you can't help but think the worst." He looked down at Orion. "Kathy really surprised me," he said. "She asked me to work with him."

That surprised me too, until I thought about it. Kathy must have felt sorry for Orion if she was breaking the RAD rules. Or maybe she was afraid that if she didn't entrust Orion to Mr. Schuster's care, she would have to have him put down.

"She said that kid who was training him isn't around anymore. You got any idea why that is?" Mr. Schuster said.

I filled him in on what had happened. I expected him to say something like, "I told you so." But he didn't. Instead he said, "That boy sure is a puzzler." I had no idea what he meant. I guess it showed on my face because he said, "He came to see me last week, after they released me from the hospital."

"Nick?" That *was* a surprise.

"I had the same reaction when I opened my front door and saw him standing there with Ed Jarvis."

I remembered seeing Nick with Mr. Jarvis in the shelter parking lot last Wednesday when my father had picked me up. They had been going somewhere together.

"At first I thought it was Ed's idea, but Ed told me, no, it was the boy who wanted to come. We sat in my living room, just me and the boy. I admit, I was suspicious. And he was uncomfortable. Boy, was he uncomfortable! For the first couple of minutes all he did was look at the floor.

I told him, you want to look at a floor, you can do that anywhere, you don't need to be in my living room."

I could imagine Nick's eyes blazing when he heard that. "What did he do?"

"You mean, what didn't he do?" Mr. Schuster said. "He didn't get mad. At first it looked like he was going to, but instead, he looked me right in the eye and told me he was sorry that he'd run into me and knocked me down and that he hadn't apologized properly. He said that he hoped slamming into me hadn't been what sent me to the hospital. Then do you know what he said?" Mr. Schuster was smiling now. "He said he knows he has an anger management problem, but that he's working on it." He chuckled. "I like that. Young boy sitting there telling me he knows he has an anger management problem."

"What did you do?" I said.

"What could I do? I accepted his apology. Then I made a pot of tea, and we talked about dogs for half an hour before Ed showed up to take him home." He reached down and scratched Orion behind the ear. "I never thought I'd say this, but he didn't seem like a bad kid. I guess it's true what they say."

I waited for him to tell me what *they* said this time.

"People aren't just one thing," he said. "You can have good, bad, and just plain stupid all in the same person." He shook his head. "I'm sorry to hear he got himself into trouble again. I think it took a lot for him to come and see me."

. . .

By mid-afternoon, I had made a decision. I drew in a deep breath and started across the lawn to the picnic table, which the RAD guys had overtaken for their break. It was practically guaranteed that they would give me a hard time. A couple of them saw me coming and nudged the rest of them. Pretty soon everyone was watching me. They all looked suspicious. I went straight to Antoine, who was sitting between Dougie and another guy whose name I didn't know.

"Can I talk to you?" I said.

Antoine looked up at me, his face impassive, as if he hadn't heard me or hadn't wanted to. For a moment I thought I was going to have to ask again. But he stood up and walked with me away from the table.

"What do you want?" he said, not friendly, but not exactly unfriendly either.

"How well do you know Nick?"

"Why?"

"What's with him and Joey?"

The question seemed to catch him off guard. "Why do you want to know about Joey?" he said.

"Do you know him?"

"I know who he is."

"He seems older than Nick."

"He's twenty. So?"

"So how come Nick's not supposed to see him?"

Antoine shrugged. "He gets into trouble whenever Joey's around. At least, that's what I heard."

"Then how come they're such good friends?"

"They're not. Joey is Nick's brother."

"His brother?" It hadn't occurred to me that Nick had a brother. He and Joey didn't look remotely like each other.

"Well, stepbrother," Antoine said. "But they were always tight, you know. Tighter than most real brothers. Nick told me one time that Joey saved his life."

"He did? How? What happened?"

"He didn't give me the details. He just mentioned it, that's all. Nick doesn't like to talk about some stuff. And he doesn't like that he can't see Joey. But he goes along with it because he wants to get out of the group home. He only had a couple of months left."

"Why do you think he did it, Antoine?"

He shrugged. "I don't know. Maybe he was bored. Or frustrated."

"Yeah, but you said Nick is always telling you not to do stupid stuff. Why would he risk more trouble by doing something as stupid as joyriding, especially when he only had a couple of months left before he could leave the group home?"

"You're asking *me?*" Antoine said. "I don't even know why *I* do what I do half the time. Like that time I kicked Jackie—I knew he wasn't the real reason I was angry. But I kicked him anyway. It's the same with most of the guys here. That's the whole point of the program. It's one of the things we're supposed to be learning. Nick's an okay guy. But nobody's perfect, right?"

It was a good answer, but it wasn't the one I wanted.

"Hey," Antoine said, after I'd started back inside. I turned to face him again. "You were right when you said you saw Nick go into that office."

"What?"

"The office where that money was," he said. "Nick went in it. But he went in to get me." He shook his head. "All that money was just lying there. I didn't think they were going to miss fifty, maybe a hundred bucks, you know?"

I waited.

"Nick saw me go inside when all that commotion was going on with that old guy. He came in and made me put the money back. He dragged me outside. He told me taking money that's supposed to help animals is the lowest thing he could think of."

I didn't say anything. But, man, did I ever wonder. A few years ago, that's exactly what Nick had done. Had he changed? Or had I been as wrong about him that time as I'd been this time?

. . .

When my father picked me up, he asked if I'd like to have supper at La Folie. It occupies the ground floor of the building my father owns. *La Folie* means "madness" in French. It was named that because the owner's wife, who is French, told him that it was *la folie* to think an upscale restaurant could succeed in what was then a mostly downscale neighborhood. She left him before the restaurant opened. My father gets to occupy the best table in the place because he bailed the owner, Fred Smith, out when Fred unexpectedly ran out of money. In exchange for "certain considerations," my father made him an interest-free loan to pay for the furniture, which arrived a mere six hours before the scheduled grand opening. The way my father worked it, he gets the back booth whenever he wants it, which is usually to impress new, big clients or when he and Vern have just wrapped up a big contract or landed a new one and want to celebrate. It works well for Fred—it brings in new repeat customers. People who experience La Folie tend to come back—again and again.

"I want to shower and change first," I said. "I'll meet you downstairs."

When I finally went down to the restaurant, I found my father and Vern sitting in what my father likes to call his booth. An open bottle of champagne sat in a bucket of ice beside the table.

"Celebrating?" I said.

My father slid over to let me sit. Vern picked up his glass and swallowed the rest of his champagne.

"I'd better get going," he said. "When I told Henri that this job involved a trip to Switzerland, well . . ." He grinned and stood up.

"You're going to Switzerland?" I said to my father.

"Not me," my father said. "Vern and Henri are going. Vern's going to set up a security system for a confidential client." He leaned close and whispered a name into my ear—the name of a big but old-time rock star. Still, I was impressed.

"Henri's hoping to collect a few autographs while we're there," Vern said. After he left, I slid into his place.

"How did you get that job?" I said.

My father shook his head as if it were no big deal. "A guy I knew in high school is the band's manager," he said. "Back then, we all thought Hal was going to sit out his life in prison on account of all the rabble-rousing he did. Who knew, huh? And the guy who was actually voted most likely to succeed? Guess what he's up to?"

I couldn't, but I bet it was going to be good.

"He went to law school, specialized in corporate law. He's doing time for major fraud. Goes to show."

Goes to show was right up there with *ironic* on the list of things my father liked to say. But he hardly ever explained what it went to show. Unlike my mother, my father is big on letting people draw their own conclusions. If he was being philosophical, he could have meant, goes to show that you can't predict someone's future based on their past. If he was thinking about his own personal life experience, he might have meant, goes to show you can't trust lawyers.

My father signaled for the waiter. "What'll it be, Robbie?" he said.

"Coke," I said. Then, because it was such a fancy restaurant, I said, "With a twist of lemon, please."

"You know, if you didn't have this forced volunteering gig, I'd have taken the job myself. You'd have liked Switzerland."

"Is that supposed to make me feel better, Dad?"

"Sorry."

The waiter set a glass of Coke in front of me. I took a sip. "You said you were going to talk to someone about Nick," I said. "Remember?"

My father patted his jacket pocket and pulled out his smartphone. He scrolled down its screen.

"Are you still not interested in this boy, Robbie?"

"No," I said. My father grinned at me. "I mean, yes," I clarified, "I'm still *not* interested. What difference does it make?"

He looked at me for a moment. "Right," he said. "Then I guess it won't upset you to learn that, according to my source, the police had a pretty good case against him when they arrested him the first time. I guess he's smart enough to know that by confessing once he was in custody—saving the police and the courts a lot of hassle—things might go a little easier for him. A little, but not much."

I swallowed hard. This did not sound good. "What exactly did your source say?"

He set aside his champagne glass and looked back at the phone's screen. "The car was reported stolen on Saturday night at eleven. But the owner isn't sure exactly when it was taken. He was visiting his mother. He parked it in the alley behind her house out near Fifth and Main at 8:00 PM."

"That's way out in the west end," I said. In fact, it was close to where Billy was working for the summer.

My father nodded. "The guy went into the house. When he went to get the car later to go home, it was gone."

"Which means that it could have been taken any time between eight and eleven," I said.

My father shook his head. "Some neighborhood kids were shooting hoops in the alley until a little after eight thirty. They all said the car was there when they left. And the accident happened . . . let's see . . ." He consulted phone. "At 9:40. So, taking into consideration where the hit-and-run happened, that means that the car must have been taken sometime between 8:40, which is just after the kids went inside and, say, 9:20 at the very latest."

"What do you mean, taking into consideration where it happened?"

"The car was taken from the west end. The hit-and-run happened in the east end, about five minutes away from where Nick's aunt lives. It would have taken at least twenty minutes to drive from where the car was originally parked to where the accident happened."

"But nobody actually saw Nick take it?"

My father gave me a peculiar look. "Robbie, he confessed. He said he did it."

"I know. And you said the police had a good case against him when they arrested him. But he didn't confess until *after* he was arrested. So if nobody saw him take the car, I was just wondering what they had on him before they made the arrest."

"Nick has a record, Robbie. That means that his fingerprints are in the system."

"*What?*"

My father misunderstood me. He started to explain what happens when people get arrested. But that wasn't what I meant.

"They found Nick's fingerprints on the car?" I said.

"Dashboard. Driver's side."

That didn't make sense. "Why would anybody with a record be stupid enough to steal a car and the leave fingerprints? Especially if he'd hit someone and hadn't stopped to help."

"Most people who do things like this aren't exactly criminal masterminds," he said—just like Morgan had predicted. "Besides, he's just a kid who went for a joy-ride. It was probably an impulse thing. In my experience, young people like Nick who get into trouble aren't usu-ally planning ahead. Mostly they're acting out."

"Acting out?"

"Working out their feelings. Like I said before, what do you actually know about this boy? There could be other things going on in his life."

"Only that he's had a lousy family life and he's been in a lot of trouble. What about the guy who was hit? Did he tell the police anything?"

"The victim, an older man, was riding his bike home. He had lights and reflectors on the bike, front and rear.

He had just stopped at a four-way stop intersection. He was starting to ride across the intersection when a car came out of nowhere—his words. He tried to get out of the way, but . . ." My father shrugged. "A pedestrian, a woman, saw the whole thing. She didn't get a good enough look at the driver to even tell if it was a man or a woman. But she saw the car. Said it was blue. She said whoever was driving didn't even slow down—they just left the guy lying in the street."

"Lying in the street?"

My father nodded. "The guy was unconscious for a couple of minutes. Besides, with a broken collarbone and a couple of broken ribs, you generally stay where you've landed."

I thought about what Nick had said when I'd run into him outside of my mother's office—that the guy had walked away. Had he been lying to me?

"In addition to the prints and the woman who described the car, they also have a witness who I.D.'d Nick as the person who abandoned the car at one thirty in the morning."

"One thirty?" I said.

My father checked his notes. "That's my information," he said. He frowned. "Seems like a long time, doesn't it?" It sure did. "If I hit a guy in a car that I had no business being in—assuming I wasn't going to stop and call the police or an ambulance—I'd be looking to ditch that car pronto. It took your friend Nick nearly four hours to get rid of it." He thought for a moment.

"Maybe he was trying to think of someplace inconspicuous to drop it. He didn't do too badly on that score. Left it at the drive-in up near Highway 10."

"They don't have drive-ins anymore, Dad," I pointed out.

"There are some still kicking around." He looked wistfully off into space for a moment. "The drive-in where Nick dropped the car isn't in operation anymore, but the screen is still there. You've seen it. We pass it when I run you up to the animal shelter."

"We do?"

"Sure. From the road it looks like a big, blank billboard. I'll point it out to you next time. I took your mother there a couple of times back before we were married." He sighed. It didn't take much imagination to guess what he was thinking about.

"And Nick left the car there?"

"Hidden behind the screen."

"But someone saw him."

"A guy out in a field across the road gave the police a positive identification."

"Some guy just happened to be in a field across the road from the drive-in in the middle of the night, and he was able to positively identify Nick? Come on, Dad!"

"Yeah, well, if it wasn't for bad luck, some people would have no luck at all, Robbie. The guy's an amateur astronomer. He was out there with his son and a telescope. They were watching for that comet, the one the papers were making such a big deal about? The guy says he saw a car weave into the old drive-in." He checked the message on his phone again. "Weave. That's what he said. When the driver got out, the guy trained his telescope on him. He said he thought maybe the guy was drunk. But that wasn't it. It turned out the driver was just a kid. The guy got a good look at him before the kid took off down the road. Then he went home and called the cops. By Monday morning they'd tied the car to the hit-and-run. Nick was arrested, and the rest you know." He looked across the table at me. "Not the way I'd want to celebrate my birthday, that's for sure."

I remembered the colorful wrapping paper and the birthday card I'd found in his backpack. "Nick got arrested on his birthday?"

"The day after. He turned sixteen on Sunday." He closed the notebook and tucked it into his pocket. "That's why he got sprung from the group home for the weekend—so he could spend the big day with his aunt. A couple of years ago, the timing would have meant a break for him for sure. Now things are different."

"What do you mean?"

"The hit-and-run happened Saturday evening. Up until a couple of years ago, if a youth under the age of sixteen committed pretty much any offense, they'd get a youth sentence, which was pretty light compared to adult sentences. Sixteen and over, for certain serious offenses, they could get an adult sentence. But that's changed. Now the magic age is fourteen. Fourteen and over, for certain crimes—basically, any crime that would result in a sentence of two years or more for an adult, and by that I mean anyone eighteen and over—the prosecution can ask for an adult sentence. The kid's lucky he's got your mother on the case. She'll probably work something out with the other attorney. She'll argue that the guy dying wasn't Nick's fault. I wouldn't be surprised if the prosecution was only pushing the negligence-causing-death charge to bargain for a serious settlement on bodily injury. But no matter how you look at it, Nick's facing more time, maybe in secure custody this time."

"Secure custody?"

"Locked up. As opposed to the group home he's in now, where he's under strict supervision and has to have permission to go out, but he's not locked up."

My phone trilled. I answered it.

"That was Mom," I said after I hung up. "She's here to pick me up. I have to go, Dad."

My father stood up. "Then by all means, let's go."

"Dad, I don't think you should—"

"Don't worry, Robbie. I'm just going to say hi."

He said considerably more than hi. He said enough to put my mother in a bad mood. Enough to make me hesitate to ask her any questions.

CHAPTER **SIXTEEN**

"I am not going to discuss this with you," my mother said as we drove home. "I shouldn't have talked to you about it in the first place. And *you* shouldn't have discussed it with your father."

"I was just trying to figure out what happened. Why he did it."

"There's nothing to figure out, Robyn. He admitted he did it. He's ready to take his punishment. It's over."

"But why was he even allowed to leave the house? His aunt was supposed to be responsible for him. Why wasn't she watching him?" If she'd been with him like she was supposed to, nothing would have happened. That man might still be alive. And Nick would be leaving the group home in a couple of months.

"He's sixteen years old, Robyn."

"But you must have asked her," I said. "He was supposed to be supervised, right? He wasn't supposed to go out alone. Right?"

My mother gave me a slightly exasperated look.

"His aunt works long shifts as a waitress," she said. "She was working on Saturday. She started at six in the morning. After her shift, she went home, made dinner, even made a cake for him, for his birthday. They had a little celebration—"

"On Saturday? But his birthday was on Sunday," I said.

My mother looked surprised. She was probably wondering how I knew when Nick's birthday was. But she didn't ask.

"He had to be back at the group home by three o'clock on Sunday afternoon," she said. "So they had the cake and presents on Saturday. His aunt rented some movies for him. Then, because she had to go on shift again at six the next morning, she made an early night of it. She went up to bed and left him downstairs watching movies."

"So she wasn't supervising him."

"It's not her fault, Robyn. This is all on Nick."

"How early?" I said.

"What?"

"You said she made an early night of it. How early?"

That earned me another exasperated look. "What difference does it make?" She shook her head. "Around eight thirty. She went upstairs a little before eight thirty. She trusted him, Robyn. That's what she told me. She trusted him to stay put."

But he hadn't. Why not?

. . .

I had an idea, but my mother didn't like it. She threw her car keys into the bowl on the table in the front hall, kicked off her shoes, and went into the kitchen to put the kettle on. While she waited for it to boil, she told me that she'd been over the incident a dozen times with Nick. He wasn't exactly communicative but that at least he hadn't tried to deny it. She said I'd be surprised how many people get caught practically red-handed and then deny they were even involved. She said maybe the RAD program really did work because Nick didn't seem angry about what happened. She said he was taking responsibility for his actions for maybe the first time in his life and that showed real maturity. She said even the police were surprised by how forth-coming he was.

"I just want to talk to him," I said.

"Robyn, this is none of your business."

"But it doesn't make sense, Mom. Everyone said he was doing so well, and then he does something incredibly stupid. It just doesn't make sense."

The look of exasperation on my mother's face changed to one of concern.

"Is there something between you and this boy?" she said.

I shook my head.

"Because if there is—"

"There isn't. I just—" Just what?

"Robyn," my mother said, her voice soft now, "do you have any idea why Nick is in that group home?"

I shook my head. I wasn't sure I wanted to hear this.

"He trashed the office at his school. Took a length of pipe and went through that place, smashing everything—computers, phones, windows, you name it. He even swung at one of the vice principals."

"Just swung?" I said. "Did he hit him?"

"No," my mother said. "But that's not the point. This boy has been in a lot of trouble."

"*Has* been. In the past."

She looked even more concerned now. The kettle started to shrill. She turned away from me to pour boiling water over herbal tea bags in two cups, one for her and one for me. She handed one to me.

"I'm only telling you this so that you'll forget about this boy, Robyn," she said. "This is not to leave this room. Do you understand me?"

I nodded.

"Something else happened on the weekend, something that Nick's aunt thinks explains why Nick did what he did."

I waited.

"On Friday night, Nick met his aunt's new boyfriend for the first time."

When his aunt had picked him up at the animal shelter, she had mentioned that she thought it was time Nick met Glen. Glen must be her boyfriend.

"Apparently it didn't go well," my mother said. "According to Nick's aunt, Nick took an instant dislike to the man. He and his aunt had a big fight about it that night. Nick's aunt thinks that's why Nick took off on Saturday night. He has trouble keeping his emotions under control. That's what gets him into trouble every time, Robyn. That's why he's in that program at the animal shelter."

I stared down into my tea. So that was the missing link, the explanation for why Nick had suddenly thrown it all away. He had lost his temper—again—and had taken his frustration out on someone else. It made sense to his aunt. It made sense to my mother.

So why didn't I want to believe it?

. . .

I couldn't sleep. I kept thinking about what Nick had done. It was so stupid. Okay, so maybe he hadn't liked his aunt's new boyfriend. But to retaliate by sneaking out and taking someone else's car? And then run into a cyclist and not even stop to see how the person was? Nick had been putting all his energy into helping to rehabilitate a dog. He was helping Antoine and the others too. How could a person who was capable of being so patient and kind also be so rash and callous?

I tossed and turned.

That wasn't the only thing that bothered me. Why had it taken Nick so long to ditch the car? It was nearly four hours from the time Nick had hit the cyclist to the time when he had been seen dumping the car. What had he been doing all that time? And why had he driven the car north, out of the city, before abandoning it? Hadn't he been worried that someone had seen the accident and could call in a description of the car? Why hadn't he just got rid of the car and run?

And what about those fingerprints? Come on. When you hit someone with a car and then flee the scene, you just know that sooner or later—probably sooner—the cops are going to be all over that car. And if you've already got a record, you know your prints are in the system. And yet he didn't think to wipe the car clean? Even if he'd panicked at first, he'd had hours to figure things out before he ditched the car.

And come to think of it, why did he go all the way across town to take a car? Why didn't he just grab something in his aunt's neighborhood?

If only his aunt had watched those videos with him. If he hadn't been alone, he wouldn't have been able to leave the house.

Okay, so my mother was right when she said it wasn't his aunt's fault. But his aunt knew Nick. She knew he was upset, and she knew how he acted when he was upset. So why had she been so trusting? Why had she left him alone at eight thirty in the evening if she thought he might be upset enough to do something crazy?

Oh.

I sat up straight in bed, staring into the darkness. Then I switched on the light, reached for my phone, and dialed my father's number.

"You know Ed Jarvis, right?" I said.

"Robbie?" My father sounded groggy. "It's nearly midnight."

"Sorry, Dad. Did I wake you?"

"Actually, yes."

"Dad, I have Nick's backpack. I found it at the animal shelter. I want to give it back to him."

There was silence on the other end of the line for a moment before my father said, "But your mother is his lawyer. Couldn't she arrange to get it back to him?"

"Please, Dad?"

"You just want to return his backpack?"

"Well, and maybe talk to him."

More silence. Then, "I'll call him in the morning. But I'm not making any promises, Robbie. Nick's in custody. There are rules about visitors."

"Thanks, Dad."

. . .

I dug up the phone book the next morning, flipped to the Ts, and looked up a number. Nick's aunt was surprised to hear from me, but she remembered who I was. She especially remembered my father. She was also surprised by my question, but she answered it. Then she said, "Are you and Nick friends?"

"He knows a lot about dogs," I said. "People at the shelter really respect him."

"Oh?" She sounded surprised. I thanked her for her time. Then I made one more phone call.

. . .

My father called me just before noon. He said he'd pick me up. I told him it was okay, I'd meet him at his place. I didn't tell him that I had to collect Nick's backpack from the closet where I'd left it.

"Correct me if I'm wrong," my father said later, when I emerged from my room, "but isn't that the same backpack you had with you when I picked you up the day before yesterday?"

"Possibly," I said.

He glanced at it again, but he didn't say another word about it.

Twenty minutes later, he pulled up to the curb in front of a large, rambling brick house on what looked like a regular residential street. Ed Jarvis was waiting for us inside.

"Thanks for bringing that over," he said, nodding at the backpack. "Nick's been frantic. He thought he'd lost it."

"I'd like to give it back to him myself," I said. "If that's okay?"

Mr. Jarvis looked at my father. My father just shrugged.

"I'll have someone bring Nick down," Mr. Jarvis said. "You can wait for him in the visiting room."

.   .   .

I was sitting at a table in a room at the back of the house. One entire wall was glass, so I saw Nick as he approached with a man. Nick looked at me. He did not smile. He came into the room. The man who was with him stood out in the hall, watching.

"Mr. Jarvis said you have something for me," he said.

I dropped his backpack onto the table. "You left it at the shelter the day you got arrested," I said.

He grabbed it, opened it and rooted through it.

"Everything's there," I said.

He zipped the pack closed again, slung it over his shoulder, and turned toward the door.

"I have a confession to make," I said.

He turned back to me.

"You know that dog book that's in there? The one that Stella gave you? I read some of it."

His eyes were hard on me, like he was trying to show me he didn't care about me or anything I had to say.

"It was really interesting," I said. He didn't say anything. "I know a few things about dogs. But I didn't know a lot of the stuff in that book."

No reaction. But then, I hadn't really expected one.

"For example," I said, "I didn't know that some things that people eat can make dogs really sick. Onions and garlic, for example. They both contain a lot of sulfur. Sulfur destroys red blood cells in dogs. Did you know that?"

He just stared at me.

"Of course you did," I said. "You underlined it in your book. Chocolate is bad for dogs too. It contains something called theobromine that can make dogs sick and even kill them. One single-serving regular chocolate bar contains enough theobromine to make a small dog very, very sick. And baking chocolate, you know, the kind used to make cakes and cookies, contains an even higher concentration. Baking chocolate can kill a dog."

"I gotta go," he said.

"Orion was sick last Sunday, Nick. Monday too."

"So?"

"So he was sick because someone gave him chocolate cake."

Still no reaction other than a frosty stare. I bet it had taken him years to perfect it.

"I saw cake crumbs and icing on his blanket, Nick. Chocolate cake and blue icing. Your aunt made your favorite cake for you on Saturday—double chocolate fudge. She wrote *Happy Birthday Nick* on it with blue icing."

Nothing.

"You went up to the animal shelter on Saturday night, didn't you? You broke in, didn't you?"

He just stared at me. It was impossible to read what he was thinking.

"The thing that doesn't make sense is why you would feed Orion chocolate cake when you knew what it would do to him."

He crossed his arms over his chest and stared at me.

"You know what I think, Nick? I think that when you told the police you hit that man with that car, you didn't know the whole story. I also think that when you said that you'd done it, no one saw any problem with that— not your aunt, not the police, not your lawyer, not even Antoine, who respects you. I mean, it's not like you're such a good guy, right, the kind of guy who never gets in trouble?"

That finally got a reaction. He glowered at me.

"But there was something that bothered me, Nick."

I waited for him to ask what it was, but he didn't.

"If you wanted to go joyriding," I said, "why did you go all the way across town to take a car? Why not find something closer to home? Closer to your aunt's home, I mean. Not closer to Joey's."

Nothing.

"Because that's where the car was taken from," I said. "Fifth and Main. I know the area. In fact, I had dinner at a restaurant near there not too long ago. It turns out that Joey and Angie live almost right across the street from the place." Angie, the very pregnant young woman I had helped down off the bus the day I'd gone to meet Billy. Angie, who had sent Nick a birthday card. Angie, in the photo with Nick and Joey. "When's the baby due?" I said. "Is that why you gave Joey money? For the baby?"

Finally—a flicker of surprise.

"How did you get from your aunt's house to where you took the car, Nick?"

Of course he didn't answer.

"You must have taken the subway and then a bus, right? I mean, how else can you have gotten across town? You don't have a car. You don't even have a driver's license. You want to know how I figure it?"

It was like talking to stone.

"Your aunt goes to bed a little before 8:30. You wait fifteen minutes or so until you're sure she's settled in for the night. Then you slip out. You take the subway and the bus up to Fifth and Main and *borrow* a car. Am I right?"

No answer.

"The only trouble is, the timing doesn't work. At that time on a Saturday night, it takes at least forty-five minutes to get from your aunt's house all the way across town to where the car was taken. I know. I called the transit authority and checked."

Nothing. No reaction.

"So say you left your aunt's house at 8:45, after you were pretty sure she was asleep. You couldn't have made it to the west end much before 9:30. But the accident happened at 9:40 back in your aunt's neighborhood. So you know what I wonder, Nick? I wonder how you got back so fast. That drive takes at least twenty minutes."

"Maybe I left earlier," he said.

"Right, you're that stupid. You slip out as soon as your aunt goes upstairs, and you just pray she won't notice."

His eyes were blazing now, but he still didn't say a word.

"That's not the only thing that doesn't add up, Nick. The guy who saw you ditch the car said you were weaving all over the road, like maybe you were drunk. But you weren't, were you? You just don't know how to drive. So how did you get all the way across town in that car at all, let alone in half the time it would take someone who knew what they were doing? And how did you get up to the animal shelter? And don't tell me you weren't there. I know you were. The cake proves it. And you ditched the car relatively close—which is something else that's been bothering me. The man was hit at 9:40, but you didn't ditch the car until nearly 1:30. How come?"

No answer.

"When I ran into you outside my—outside your lawyer's office, you told me it was no big deal, that the guy you hit walked away. But he didn't walk away, Nick. He didn't even get up. He couldn't. That isn't what Joey told you, is it? Joey made it sound like it wasn't such a big deal, right?"

He finally cracked—a little.

"Joey's got nothing to do with this," he said.

"Yeah? Well, I think he does. And I think you're covering for him. I don't know why. Maybe you think you owe him. Maybe you think this is no big deal for you, but it would be a much bigger deal for him. He's older. He's had his driver's license suspended, hasn't he?" I'd remembered what Nick had said when he'd used my phone to call Joey, and what Joey had said when I'd caught him at the fence with Nick. Joey had been waiting to get his license back.

Nick's façade slipped. Now he looked really surprised.

"A suspended license means that he's already been in big trouble. If you confessed to a hit-and-run while joy-riding, you'd probably get some more time in custody. Maybe you'd get lucky. Maybe you'd serve your time at the group home. Maybe you wouldn't get locked up. But Joey's twenty. If he were to be convicted, he'd be locked up for sure. Especially if he was driving while his license was suspended. And if he's been involved in something like this before. Has he, Nick?"

He just looked at me.

"Except the guy died," I said. "You could get worse now."

He spun around and headed for the door.

"Fine," I said, standing up. "You stick to your story, and I'll stick to mine. But you know what, Nick? The police are going to believe me, not you. You know why? Because I'm not a screw–up like you!"

He whirled back.

"Shut up," he said. "Just shut up, okay?"

"No," I said. "I'm going to tell them everything I know. And they're going to see that your story doesn't make sense. You can try to cover for Joey, but they're going to get him. Wait and see."

His hands were clenched into fists now. I glanced at the man who was standing out in the hall. I don't think he could hear us, but he was watching Nick intently.

"Come on, Nick. Be smart," I said. "You accepted responsibility for what happens to Orion. You can help him. You already have helped him, but he may not make it without you.

"You helped Antoine too. He told me. You stopped him from taking that money. But covering for Joey? He's going to be a father soon. He should be taking responsibility for himself. You're not helping him by letting him get away with it."

"Why can't you just stay out of this?" he said.

"Because what Joey did is wrong. And what you're doing isn't helping him, but it is hurting you." I stared into his eyes. "Do you really want people to think you did this?" He glared at me. "Antoine told me that Joey saved your life. Is that why you're covering for him?"

No answer. He was the most unresponsive person I had ever met. Maybe that's how he was dealing with his anger now—by trying to keep it all bottled up inside him.

I walked past him to the door and reached for the doorknob.

"My stepfather," Nick said. "Joey's father? He was real mean."

I turned to look at him.

"He drank. And he used to hurt my mother. One time he had a knife. He was threatening her with it. I tried to stop him. But he's a really big guy and I was just a kid. If Joey hadn't stopped him, he would have killed me for sure." He touched the scar that ran across his cheek. "He attacked Joey instead. Joey almost died." He looked at me. "The absolute worst they can do to me is two years. My lawyer even said so. Even two years in closed detention, that's not so bad. I'll be eighteen when I get out. The record will be sealed. Joey's twenty. He has two drunk driving arrests. They'd do a lot worse to him. They'd really mess things up for him. And the baby's due soon."

"*They're* not going to mess him up," I said. "He's done this to himself. And he's going to let you take the blame for it."

"I owe him."

"You don't owe him this. Nick, if you don't tell your lawyer, I will."

Nick sank down onto a chair. "You're a real pain, you know that?" he said.

I sat down opposite him. "What really happened that night?"

He shook his head. I waited.

"Joey showed up at the house after my aunt went to bed," Nick started. "He snuck in. Joey can get in anywhere. He'd been drinking. Celebrating, he said. You know, my birthday. He wanted me to go with him. He said he had a surprise for me. He grabbed the rest of the cake and we went. I know it was stupid, but it was Joey. Besides, who else was going to know?"

I nodded.

"He had a car I'd never seen before. He said he'd borrowed it, but he didn't say who from. He told me he'd just got his license back too. I asked him where we were going, but he kept saying it was a surprise. The next thing I know, we're up behind the shelter and Joey's jimmying the lock on a door to the animal wing. I tried to stop him, but he said, 'Hey, it's your birthday. You want to see that dog, don't you? You want to introduce me to him, don't you?' He said if I wanted to, we could even take Orion with us. Then the door was open and . . ." He shrugged and looked down at the floor.

I waited.

"He went in and I followed him," Nick said. He sounded ashamed now. "And the next thing I know, Joey's inside the kennel and he's feeding Orion some cake. Orion gobbled it up before I could get in and stop him. I just knew it was going to make him sick."

He glanced up at me. For the first time, he looked sorry.

"I told Joey we had to get out of there. So we took off, back to the car. And that's when he told me. The whole thing. The big surprise. The whole reason he'd showed up." His voice was bitter. "It wasn't because it was my birthday. I don't think he even remembered that until he saw the cake my aunt had made. It was because he was in trouble again. He'd lost his job, you know, on account of they'd taken away his driver's license. He was having trouble getting hired anywhere, and he and Angie were behind on their rent. The baby is due soon and he was under so much pressure . . . He said he couldn't take it. He had a few drinks. Then he borrowed a car—he said he wanted to see me. He said it's not fair that I'm not supposed to see him. But he hit some guy, and he got scared. He said he wanted me to help him ditch the car. But mostly he wanted me to help him out of the whole thing. He said the guy walked away, but he thought someone saw him. There was a woman. He said nothing would probably ever come of it, but if it did, maybe I could do something for him. One last time, you know? I was going to say no. But he begged me. He talked about the baby. He loves Angie. He really does. And he has a line on a job."

He sighed. "I ditched the car. I thought I wiped off all the prints. I guess I missed a couple, huh?"

I nodded. I didn't know what else to say.

"His kid deserves to have a father around," Nick said. "Even if it's Joey. Maybe he'll straighten out. You know?"

I nodded, even though I wasn't so sure.

He leaned forward in his chair. "I don't get you," he said.

"I don't get you, either." Man, was that the truth.

"Are you really going to tell the cops?"

I nodded.

"I'm still going to be in trouble, you know," he said. "For helping Joey."

"I know."

For a few moments, neither of us said anything. Nick looked at me, but he didn't try to argue. I started to get up. My father was probably wondering what was taking me so long. But . . .

"Can I ask you something, Nick?"

"Man, you're worse than the cops." He gave me a wry smile. "All right. Go ahead."

Thanks to my mother, I knew what he'd done. But I didn't know why. Suddenly it seemed important.

"What are you doing in RAD?"

He shrugged. At first I thought that was all the answer I was going to get. It wasn't.

"I kind of went crazy at school one day," he said.

"How come?"

"He killed her," he said. At first I didn't get it. "My stepfather. The last time he started in on my mother, he killed her. They plea-bargained it down to manslaughter. He got eight years, eligible for parole in three. Three lousy years." His purple-blue eyes burned as he looked at me. "A couple of weeks later, I got sent down to the office, to this vice principal. He was new. It was maybe his first week there. There was this school secretary. She was always nice to me—she was nice to all the kids, it didn't matter where they came from. She told him that he should go easy on me because of what happened to my mother. The guy, the *vice principal*, had my file in his hands. I could tell he'd read it, and he'd already made up his mind about me.

You know what he said to the secretary, while I was standing right there?"

I shook my head. But I had a bad feeling.

"He said that any woman who would stay with a man who beat on her pretty much deserved whatever happened to her."

"Oh . . ." I tried to put myself in his place. I tried to think what I would have done.

"He said it to the secretary. Maybe he didn't mean for me to hear it. But I did." He shook his head. "There was a janitor or plumber or something working on the overhead pipes in the office. I grabbed the first thing I saw"—a length of pipe, according to my mother—"and, well . . ." He looked down at the ground.

"What happened to the vice principal?" I said. "I hope they at least fired him for what he said."

He raised his head and looked at me as though I were crazy.

"You're kidding, right?" he said. "Fire a vice principal?"

"It happens," I said.

"Yeah, well, it didn't happen to this guy."

The man out in the hall rapped on the glass. Nick stood up and slung his backpack over one shoulder.

"I gotta go," he said.

There was just one more thing I had to ask, one more thing I needed to know.

"When you stole the money from school, that was Joey with you, wasn't it?"

He nodded.

"Antoine said you tried to stop him from taking that money at the shelter. Were you trying to stop Joey too?"

Nick met my eyes and held them. At first he looked angry. But by the time he finally shook his head, he looked ashamed. "No," he said. "I was there to steal the money."

I don't know why I was so disappointed. I guess I was hoping that I'd been wrong about him all along.

"I wanted a dog so badly," he said. "I've always wanted one. My stepdad finally said he'd let me get one if I could pay for its food. I thought maybe I could get a part-time job. Then Joey saw the posters for that pet show when he picked me up after school. He figured maybe there was an easier way to get what I needed." He shook his head. "They told me you and your friends worked hard to raise that money."

"They told me you blew it all at an arcade downtown."

"Yeah." He shook his head. "Turns out my stepdad only said I could have the dog because he never thought I'd come up with the money. When I showed him the cash, he just laughed." The hurt was visible in his eyes, even after all this time. "Joey said we might as well have some fun."

The man out in the hall rapped on the glass and nodded at the door.

"I better go," Nick said. Then, as he reached for the doorknob, he said, "I'm sorry, Robyn."

CHAPTER **SEVENTEEN**

S ix days later, it was my last day at the shelter. I had been looking over my shoulder all day. I knew, because my mother had told me, that Joey had been arrested shortly after I'd talked to Nick at the group home. I also knew that with the help of Mr. Jarvis, Kathy, and Mr. Schuster, she had succeeded in getting the charges against Nick dropped and had arranged for a meeting between Nick and the chairman of the shelter's board. Kathy thought that if the chairman had a chance to talk to Nick, he might change his mind about banishing him from the shelter. The meeting was supposed to happen today. I hoped that it would go well and that Nick would be allowed to return. But I dreaded running into him. Joey was definitely looking at some time in jail. I wondered if Nick blamed me for that. I was almost positive that if I hadn't threatened to tell, he would never have told my mother what really happened and Joey would never have been arrested.

I stayed in my broom closet of an office and kept my eyes on my computer screen all day. I didn't even go outside for lunch. Then, at four o'clock, Kathy knocked on my door and said she needed me to do one last thing for her.

"We're having a reception for some of our donors this evening," she said. "Janet could use some help setting up. She's in the boardroom."

So was everyone else I had gotten to know over the past month. And they all yelled, "Surprise!" when I entered the room. Kathy laughed when she saw the expression on my face.

"We wanted to thank you for all your hard work, Robyn," she said. "Because of you, we now have an up-to-date fund-raising database. I know it was tedious work, but it means a lot to us."

Everyone smiled and clapped. Then Kathy cut pieces of chocolate cake for everyone and presented me with a gift. Everyone I had worked with over the past month told me how much they had appreciated my efforts. I felt pretty good about what I had done, even though I hadn't really wanted to be there in the first place.

I was on my way back to my office after the party to get my things when I saw Nick emerge from a meeting room. He was more dressed up than usual, in gray pants, a neatly pressed shirt, and shoes instead of sneakers, and he was almost, but not quite, smiling. Mr. Jarvis was with him. So was Orion.

I was about to duck around a corner out of sight when Nick spotted me. He said something to Mr. Jarvis, handed him Orion's leash, and started down the hall toward me. I stood where I was, too embarrassed to run away but a little afraid of what he might say to me.

What he said was "Hi."

"Hi," I said.

We looked at each other.

"They were going to kick me out of the program," he said finally. "But Kathy and Mr. Jarvis convinced them to give me another chance. Mr. Schuster too. And my lawyer."

"That's good," I said.

His eyes held me. The way he was looking at me, like he was trying to look into me, made me want to turn and run.

"Why didn't you tell me that my lawyer is your mother?" he said.

"I thought you wouldn't talk to me if you knew."

"Yeah," he said. "You're probably right." He glanced back over his shoulder at Mr. Jarvis, who was waiting for him. "So I guess she told you what happened with Joey, huh?"

I nodded. "I'm sorry," I said.

"Me too. Angie was really upset. But I think maybe she'll give him another chance when he gets out. I sure hope he doesn't mess it up."

"Me, too," I said.

The silence that followed was awkward. Nick rushed to fill it.

"Mr. Jarvis and Stella say that if I work hard, Orion and I can probably graduate the program with everyone else. He's a little behind, but Mr. Schuster worked with him while I was away, so at least he hasn't forgotten everything I taught him."

"I'm glad."

I looked past him at Mr. Jarvis and Orion. Both were patiently watching us.

"Well, I guess I'd better go," I said. "It's my last day here."

"Oh?" Was I imagining it, or did he sound disappointed? "So you're out of here?"

I nodded.

We looked at each other for a few uncomfortable moments. "Well, good-bye," I said at last. I turned to go.

"Hey, Robyn," he said. "I was wondering . . ."

I waited.

"When Orion and me graduate . . . I mean, *if* we graduate, I was wondering . . . there's going to be a sort of graduation ceremony here. We're allowed to invite some guests. You think maybe you'd like to come? As my guest?"

"Me?"

"Yeah."

"Well . . ." I can't say I hesitated long before I answered. "Okay. Sure."

He smiled at me. Nick D'Angelo actually smiled at me. He glanced back over his shoulder.

"There's one thing you have to do before you leave," he said. "It'll just take a minute."

"What is it?"

"Come on." He started back toward Mr. Jarvis and Orion. I trailed behind him, reluctant to get too close to the big dog.

Nick took the dog's leash from Mr. Jarvis.

"Come on," he said again.

I followed him outside onto the lawn where he got Orion to sit.

"It's about time you two became friends," Nick said. "I wouldn't be here if it wasn't for you. And if I wasn't here, I don't know what would happen to Orion. Give me your hand." I extended my hand, and he took it gently in his. His palm was callused but warm, and I felt a tingle go up my arm. Slowly he brought both his hand and mine closer to Orion. The big dog looked up at me but remained seated. His nostrils quivered as he sniffed my scent. "He likes it when you scratch him behind the ears," Nick said. He guided my hand to the top of the big dog's head and nodded to encourage me. I scratched the big dog's head gingerly. Almost immediately, Orion's tail started to thump happily against the ground. Nick smiled at me again. I'd never seen him look so happy. I felt like I'd just made two new friends.

"We were working on a project together. But she didn't get a lot done, probably because her mother is so sick. I could have been nice about it, but I wasn't." Nick looked at me strangely. I couldn't make myself meet his eyes. "That same day, she took off."

#1 *Last Chance*

Robyn's scared of dogs—like, really scared. But she agrees to spend her summer working at an animal shelter anyway. (It's a long story.) Robyn soon discovers that many juvenile offenders also volunteer at the shelter—including Nick D'Angelo, a boy from Robyn's past. A boy she hoped to never see again.

Nick has a talent for getting into trouble, but after his latest arrest, Robyn suspects that he just might be innocent. And she sets out to prove it. . . .

#2 *You Can Run*

Trisha Hanover has run away from home before. But this time, she hasn't come back. To make matters worse, Robyn blew up at Trisha the same morning she disappeared. Now Robyn feels responsible, and she sets out to track Trisha down.

As Robyn follows Trisha's path, she learns some harsh truths about the runaway's life. And when she finally locates Trisha, Robyn also finds herself in danger.

#3 *Nothing to Lose*

Robyn is excited to hang out with her sorta-boyfriend Nick after weeks apart. Nick has a dark history, but Robyn's sure he has reformed—until she notices suspicious behavior during their trip to Chinatown.

Turns out Nick's been doing favors for dangerous people. Robyn urges him to stop, but the situation might be out of her control—and Nick's. . . .

ABOUT THE AUTHOR

Norah McClintock is the author of several mystery series for teenagers, and a five-time winner of the Crime Writers of Canada's Arthur Ellis Award for Best Juvenile Crime Novel. McClintock was born and raised in Montreal, Quebec. She lives in Toronto with her husband and children.